TOO MANY TOPPINGS!

TOO MANY TOPPINGS!

Coco Simon

Simon Spotlight

New York   London   Toronto   Sydney   New Delhi

SIMON SPOTLIGHT
An imprint of Simon & Schuster Children's Publishing Division
1230 Avenue of the Americas, New York, New York 10020
This Simon Spotlight edition February 2019
Copyright © 2019 by Simon & Schuster, Inc.
All rights reserved, including the right of reproduction in whole or in part in any form.
SIMON SPOTLIGHT and colophon are registered trademarks of Simon & Schuster, Inc.
For information about special discounts for bulk purchases, please contact
Simon & Schuster Special Sales at 1-866-506-1949 or business@simonandschuster.com.
Text by Caroline Smith Hickey
Series designed by Hannah Frece
Cover designed by Alisa Coburn and Hannah Frece
Cover illustrations by Alisa Coburn
The text of this book was set in Bembo Std.
Manufactured in the United States of America 0119 OFF
10 9 8 7 6 5 4 3 2 1
ISBN 978-1-5344-3651-0 (hc)
ISBN 978-1-5344-3650-3 (pbk)
ISBN 978-1-5344-3652-7 (eBook)
Library of Congress Catalog Card Number 2018948331

CHAPTER ONE

LATE AGAIN

I checked the time on my phone as I hurried down the sidewalk—1:12 p.m. Whoops! I was late for my most important, most favorite activity of the week. Well, *one* of my most favorite activities. I had a lot of favorites. That was sort of the problem.

"I'm late! I know! I'm sorry!" I declared as I burst through the front door of Molly's Ice Cream parlor. The bell tied to the top of the door tinkled merrily, but that was the only merry thing that greeted me. My two best friends, Allie Shear and Tamiko Sato, were both in a whir of activity, taking orders and scooping ice cream.

Tamiko glanced up and gave me an icy stare, colder even than the ice cream. Ouch.

Even the customers in line seemed annoyed. Maybe I shouldn't have announced my lateness quite so . . . loudly.

I quickly tied back my long, curly brown hair and wished I'd thought of that on the way there. Customers didn't want hair in their food, and they probably didn't want to see me tying it back as I was dashing to the counter!

As quick as a flash, I washed my hands, donned an apron and a huge smile, and took my place at the register. I was the best at math, so I usually took the money and made change, while Tamiko, master marketeer, took orders and tried to convince customers to choose exciting new options that she often invented on the spot. Allie, whose mother owned the store, made the cones and shakes. We all did a little bit of everything, truth be told, but the three of us had been working together every Sunday afternoon for a few months now, and we'd gotten into a very comfortable and efficient rhythm of who did what.

There was no chance to explain my lateness with customers waiting. But with all three of us pitching in, we made quick work of the line and soon had the shop to ourselves. I took the opportunity to wipe down the counters, paying extra attention to the area around the toppings bar.

I felt really bad about being late. I wanted to apologize, but I was scared to bring it up because I knew Tamiko and Allie would be mad. And I *hated* when my friends were mad at me. I was pretty sure I hated that feeling more than any other feeling in the world.

"Today must be your lucky day," Tamiko said finally.

I could hear the edge in her voice. It made my stomach queasy.

"What's lucky about being late?" I asked. I knew it was better to just say it than to try to pretend it hadn't happened.

"You're lucky because we were low on rainbow sprinkles, and my mom ran out to the store to get more before you got here," Allie explained. Her voice was less edgy, but I could tell she was annoyed too. "So she won't know you were late. Because we won't tell her."

"Yeah," said Tamiko. "You'll get away with it. Again."

The bad feeling in my stomach grew worse. I

didn't like getting away with something. I wasn't *trying* to get away with anything. I really wasn't.

"Thanks for understanding, you guys," I said. "I really do have a good excuse! My soccer game yesterday got canceled because of the rain and rescheduled for this morning. And then the game was 3–3, so we went into overtime. . . . "

Allie sighed and rubbed a gritty spot on the counter with her thumbnail. "That's the problem, Sierra. You *always* have a good excuse."

"Since when is having a good excuse a bad thing?" I asked. I half smiled, trying to bring a little cheerfulness to the situation. After all, we were only talking about twelve minutes. Twelve minutes! I didn't *technically* have to be there until one o'clock. I was sometimes much later for things.

Allie glanced at Tamiko. They seemed to have an entire conversation with their eyes in mere seconds.

Then Allie said, "Because I'm waiting for the day when you tell somebody *else* that the reason you need to leave early is because you have a responsibility to be at your job at Molly's. Which my mom pays you for. Why is everything else more important to you than being here?"

"It isn't more important!" I protested. "Really. I love my job here—you know that. I'm just, well . . . I guess I'm just so used to being late that this isn't really that late to me. Anyway, I figured you guys would understand."

"We do understand—you're taking advantage of your friends," Tamiko said. "And it's not cool, Sierra."

Wow. Another ouch. This day was just getting worse and worse. Tamiko was always outspoken and said exactly what was on her mind, which I loved about her. But occasionally, when it was directed at me (or at one of my faults), it could hurt a little. But I couldn't deny that it was true: I did count on our friendship to keep me from getting into too much trouble. Working at Molly's on Sundays was my job. I needed to take it just as seriously as soccer, and softball, and student council, and all the other things I did. Because they were all commitments I had made. And even more important, they were all so much *fun*. That's why I committed to so many things in the first place. I loved activities, and meeting new people, and being involved in lots of stuff. It made my head spin, but in a really good and exciting way. I was not the type of person to sit around. I liked to *go, go, go*!

5

Sometimes it was hard to explain that to people who liked things calm and structured, like Allie. Or precise and efficient, like Tamiko.

"Listen, you guys. I am really, really, *really,* truly, with cherries and Oreos and sprinkles on top, sorry. Okay? I'll stay later today to make up the time."

Allie sighed. "I know, Sierra. It's just that you've said that before."

Just then Allie's mom, Mrs. Shear, breezed in. "I'm back, girls!" she called, her arms full of economy-size tubs of toppings. "And they had so many yummy-looking things at the store that I had to try a few new things."

She went straight for the toppings bar and showed us the spiced nuts, lemon curd, nut brittle, and pepper-mint she'd bought. "Tamiko," she said, "I'll leave you in charge of coming up with interesting new treats that use these. You always have good ideas."

She patted Tamiko on the shoulder and flashed me a smile as she headed toward the back of the shop, where the storage and little office area were. We all called it "backstage."

"Now, I'll be backstage for a while doing some paperwork, but feel free to come back if you need to talk to me," Mrs. Shear said. "And, Allie, please put some music on. . . . It's dead in here!"

Allie obediently turned on the store's speaker system and cued up a song on her phone. It was a fast-paced song and sounded out of place as my two friends and I stared at one another, not sure how to go on after our disagreement, especially since Allie's mom was back and might overhear us.

I was grateful they hadn't told on me, and truly sorry for being late. But I believed I had a valid excuse. I played right fullback on my soccer team, and my sub hadn't been there. I'd *had* to play. But there were *two* other employees here at Molly's working, and both were able to do the cash register. Was there something else they were mad about? Or was it really just my occasional lateness?

The three of us worked for a while in stony silence. Allie and Tamiko were stiff and awkward, and I felt so miserable that I debated whether I should just go tell Mrs. Shear I'd been twelve minutes late so that she could reprimand me. Maybe then my friends would let me off the hook. But if Allie had wanted her mother to know, she would have told her, and she hadn't. So I didn't want to get *her* in trouble for covering for me.

Ugh. It was all so awkward.

Finally an older lady came in and began studying the menu.

"What can I get you?" asked Tamiko, turning on her special Molly's charm. "We have lots of one-of-a-kind treats that aren't on the menu, so just tell me what you're in the mood for, and I'll make it happen!"

The woman, who was wearing a beautiful print scarf and pearls, looked amused. "One of a kind?"

Allie jumped in. "Yes! Here at Molly's all of our ice cream is homemade, and we constantly have new items on the menu that you can't find anywhere else. Molly's is completely unique."

"I like unique." The woman smiled, studying us. "Are you three friends, or just coworkers?"

"Friends," I said quickly. "Best friends. They're my two best friends in the whole world."

The woman nodded knowingly. "I have two best friends too. We've known each other since we were kids. Three can be a hard number for friendships sometimes, but I'm glad to see you girls have it all worked out."

I didn't say anything, and neither did Allie or

Tamiko. I wasn't sure we had it *all* worked out, especially today.

"I have a good feeling about you girls," the woman said. "How about you surprise me with something of your choice?"

Tamiko clapped her hands with joy and, with a sly look at me, whispered something into Allie's ear. Allie nodded and quickly got to work.

Tamiko told me what to charge, and I rang it up on the cash register. When Allie presented the woman with the finished product, a frothy milkshake made with three scoops of vanilla ice cream, flavored with spiced nuts, lemon curd, and peppermint.

"Mmm. It looks heavenly," the woman said. "What's it called?"

Tamiko beamed. "It's called a forgiveness float. Because even though friendships can sometimes be spicy or sour, forgiveness is sweet."

The woman took a sip and beamed. "Well done, girls. This tastes exactly like forgiveness—especially the little bit of lemon curd!"

She slipped a five-dollar bill into our tip jar and gave me a wink as she walked out the door.

"Thanks, you guys," I said, relieved to have been forgiven. "I mean it."

"You're welcome," said Allie. "Just don't make the forgiveness float a permanent item on the menu, okay?"

"Yeah," Tamiko agreed. "Promise us you won't add one more thing to your schedule, Sierra. You can't handle it, and we can't either."

I nodded vigorously. "I won't! I pinky-swear promise."

The three of us linked pinkies, and just like that, the day got better.

CHAPTER TWO

PLANNING AHEAD

The next night, I was sitting at the dinner table with my parents, waiting for my sister. My family had a rule about not eating until everyone was present, so we were just waiting and waiting, with all of my dad's delicious homemade Cuban cooking sitting in front of us, getting cold.

"Isabel!" Mom called. "*¡Ahora!* Now!"

I heard heavy footsteps on the stairs, and then a minute later Isa appeared in the doorway of the dining room. She was dressed in black from head to toe: black tights, black skirt, and a washed-out black T-shirt. Her expression was black too, like thunderclouds. I guess she'd been doing something pretty interesting up in her room. Not that I'd know what it was, since these days Isa and I hardly knew what the other one was doing.

It was kind of weird, especially considering the fact that we were identical twins.

"Who died, Isa?" I asked, trying to lighten the mood. I knew my parents were annoyed that she'd kept us waiting, and I was pretty sure her all-black ensemble would irk them too.

"Who died?" Isa repeated, giving *my* outfit—a bright yellow sweater, a jean skirt, and yellow socks—a withering look. "Your fashion sense. Obviously."

"Girls!" said Mom. "Not at dinner." She glanced at Dad and sighed. "Do you remember when they were little, and I had to fight to get them to wear different outfits, because they always wanted to dress exactly the same?" She shook her head in disbelief.

Dad laughed. "I do remember. They were the two cutest things I'd ever seen. And I've delivered baby bunny rabbits."

Mom and Dad were both vets and ran a veterinary hospital together, so they always had great animal stories.

"The days of Sierra and me looking alike are long gone," said Isa, more cheerfully now. "Thank goodness." Then she looked pointedly at me. "Hey, Sunshine, can you pass me the salad?"

My face broke into a grin. Even when Isa really annoyed me, and lately it was often, I had to appreciate her sense of humor. Calling me "Sunshine" because of my bright yellow sweater was pretty funny.

"Are either of you girls available to help at the hospital tomorrow after school? We're going to be a little short-staffed and might need an extra pair of hands."

"My science teacher is offering a special study session after school tomorrow to help kids prepare for our test next week," said Isa. "I need to go."

"And I've got my first rehearsal for the school play," I said. "Sorry. Maybe I can help you guys another day?"

Mom frowned. "I'm still not sure how I feel about you doing the play, Sierra. You've already got too much going on. Not to mention your regular schoolwork, which you need to keep up with. School has to come first, and with the play it all seems like a bit too much."

I forced myself to keep my voice calm. My parents didn't like it when anyone got hysterical at dinner. "I understand, Mom, but I'm the lighting director for the play. I've already agreed to do it. And anyway, the show is in just a few weeks, and then it'll be over, so that'll be one less thing on my plate. Okay?"

Dad glanced down at my plate, which was still mostly full. "Right now I wish you'd eat a little something off *that* plate," he joked. "I worked hard on that *ropa vieja*!"

Dad's *ropa vieja*, which was Cuban-style shredded beef, was usually one of my favorites. But for some reason I just wasn't hungry this evening. I'd gotten home late from school because of softball, and I knew I had a long night of homework ahead of me. I felt all jumpy inside, and nervous, the way I did when I knew I had a lot to do and hadn't figured out yet how to do it all.

"Sorry, Dad," I said. "I guess I'm just a little distracted."

"Maybe the glare of your sweater is making you queasy," Isa suggested.

I rolled my eyes at her and made myself take a huge bite of the *ropa vieja*, then said, "MMMMMMmmmm," really loudly to make Dad feel better.

"If you're too distracted to eat," said Dad, "then

you definitely need to rethink your schedule, Sierra. I don't think there's ever been a day in my life when I've been too distracted to eat!"

"Me neither," said Mom, squinting her eyes at me now and looking worried. "I really think you should—"

"Don't worry, Mami! I have everything under control. I promise. How about I go right up after dinner to do homework and organize my week, okay? I'll show you my planner, and then I can prove to you that I can get it all done."

"*Sí, sí.* That's a good idea. But I'm going to be keeping an eye on you. If I see you starting to look too stressed, we're going to have another talk. Deal?"

"Deal!" I agreed quickly, even though I couldn't believe how much everyone in my family was worrying. I was perfectly fine! This was just how I did things. It might not work for other people, but it worked for me. I liked keeping busy.

After dinner I plopped down onto my bed with my backpack and school planner. I started filling in all the things I had to do that week, from lighting rehearsals, to sports practices, to Molly's, to homework. I

15

hummed as I worked, which Isa always made fun of me for, but I couldn't help it. When I was concentrating or daydreaming, I hummed. During tests, during soccer games, even when I was watching TV sometimes! I sang in the shower too. I guess I had to always be doing *something*, and music was another thing that I loved.

After about fifteen minutes of moving things around in my planner, I made it all fit. I even slotted in time to study for that science test Isa had mentioned. We were in different sections but had the same test. She has even even let me use her notes from the next day's special study session when I offered to do a few chores for her.

I really could get everything done! I wanted to rush downstairs and show my mother. But then my eyes fell onto a paper I had tucked into the folder pocket of my planner. It was the student council meeting schedule, and there was one the next day after school. There was no way I could make it, and I was the student council secretary. I had to be there to take notes.

Hurriedly I grabbed my phone and began texting everyone on the council, trying to find an alternate time to meet. I knew it was a big inconvenience, but hopefully everyone would understand. The play would be over soon, so this wouldn't affect the next council meeting.

After a lot of back-and-forth, and a few very snippy texts from the treasurer, we arranged to meet the next morning before school instead of after. I'd have to get up really early, which meant I couldn't study as much as I'd like for the science test tonight, but I'd still get to do everything.

I wanted to text Allie and Tamiko and tell them what I'd just done, and how I'd worked everything out without letting anyone down or making anyone late, but I didn't. I had more work to do first.

I focused on my homework and double-checked my planner twice to make sure I had included everything I needed to get to this week. I was ready to turn over a new leaf. I was going to still do all the things that I loved *and* get to them on time—because I really couldn't bear the idea of dropping even a single activity.

Playing softball and soccer made me happy because I loved both games (not to mention my teammates), and student council was a great way to have a say in how our school was run, and last year's play had been so much fun! Everyone had joked around backstage and played pranks. And opening nights were spectacular. I didn't want to miss it this year. And Molly's—well, that was not just a way to earn a little money but also quality time with my two best friends.

Everything I did was part of who I was—yellow-sweater-wearing, humming, sunshiny Sierra. And I wasn't going to give any of it up. And I didn't have to! I just couldn't add any more, like Tamiko had said.

As I was climbing into bed, I texted Allie and Tamiko. Good night, girls! I just scheduled my whole week in advance. I'm learning! You'll see!

Allie texted back right away: Yay! Glad to hear it.

Tamiko didn't respond. As I was closing my eyes, I told myself she was probably just studying, or working hard on some art project. She was always bedazzling or redesigning something. Maybe I should ask her to help me redo my room.

No, Sierra! said a little voice in my head. *No more projects for now!*

Everyone was yawning. Claire Bright, the student council president, yawned as she opened the meeting with the gavel. Vice President Vikram Kapoor yawned and stretched, and accidentally knocked his lunch bag off the table, spilling its contents all over the floor. And Treasurer Lee Murphy actually glared at me *while yawning*, as I uncapped my pen to begin taking notes.

I knew that seven o'clock in the morning was early to be at school for a meeting, but it wasn't the end of the world. And it was only once, right?

"Sorry, guys!" I said again, even though I'd already apologized when we'd first arrived. The custodian, Mr. Lewis, had had to let us into the school because we were so early. He'd raised his eyebrows at us and pointed toward the math wing, where he'd already mopped the floors, indicating we could use one of those classrooms. "It's just for today, okay?" I told the group.

"I needed to study for Spanish this morning," Lee grumbled. "I have a HUGE test later today."

"Yeah, and I had to get my mom to drive me because the bus doesn't come this early, and she was mad," said Vikram. "She had to bring my two little sisters along, and they were still in pj's, and she had to get them ready for school and go to work."

Claire, who was usually calm and unflappable, heaved a sigh. "We're all tired, thanks to Sierra. But let's try to have a productive meeting anyway, okay? Sierra, can you read the minutes from last meeting, please? And can you add something to this meeting's notes about never having a before-school meeting again? Let's put it in the bylaws."

I wanted to crawl under the table. Was it really *that* bad to have had to come to school early for one morning? Weren't they used to being flexible and juggling a few things at the same time?

Maybe not. Maybe none of them were juggling as many things as I was, and that's why this seemed like such a big deal. I was the kind of person who rolled with the punches, but I knew not everyone was like that.

I stopped myself from apologizing yet again and began reading the previous meeting's notes. We had a job to do. But I did make a mental note that not everyone was going to bend over backward to accommodate my schedule. And I would make sure to put the rest of the year's student council meetings in permanent marker in my planner as soon as possible.

"First on the agenda," said Claire, suppressing another yawn. "Spring fair. I vote for a sleepathon."

"I second the motion," said Lee.

It was a relief to get to lunch and see Tamiko and our other friend MacKenzie, who was new to Martin Luther King Middle School and sat with us a lot. She hadn't replaced Allie as our third *amiga*, but she was really nice and fun. And I always thought, the more the merrier, anyway. Especially in the cafeteria.

All three of us had bought lunch today, and unfortunately, it was mac and cheese. Most schools could make a decent mac and cheese (how hard was pasta with cheese, seriously?), but not MLK. Our lunch was both gluey and gritty, which were two things that no one felt like tasting after a long morning of learning.

MacKenzie stabbed at her lunch with her fork. "I need to get up earlier," she said. "My mom says she's done packing lunches for me, so if I don't want to eat the school's lunch, I need to pack one myself. But today I hit the snooze button."

"How long is your snooze button?" Tamiko asked. "It doesn't take *that* long to pack a lunch."

MacKenzie grinned. "Well, I hit it, like, four times. . . ."

We all laughed, then looked dejectedly at our lunches again.

"Speaking of early," I said, "I had to drag the whole student council in this morning to meet because I've got my first lighting rehearsal after school. I think they're all really mad at me. Lee Murphy won't even talk to me."

MacKenzie shook her head. "They shouldn't be mad at you! It's their job. Right?"

"It's their job to meet *after* school, not before," said Tamiko. "It's Sierra's job to make sure she can do all the things she's promised to, not make everyone else work around her."

MacKenzie's eyes flashed sympathy at me, and she seemed to wait to see if I was going to respond.

"I made it work," I said, keeping my voice even and calm. I felt stung by Tamiko's words but didn't want to overreact. She always spoke bluntly, and generally didn't mean things quite the way they sounded. And I was probably sensitive about it anyway because of our fight the other day. But since Tamiko had been the one to come up with the forgiveness float, I was pretty sure that deep down everything was okay.

Tamiko appeared not to notice my discomfort or MacKenzie's sympathy. Instead she held her phone up at a strategic angle to get a picture of our lunches. "I'm going to send this to Allie. I bet they're not eating this glop over at Vista Green."

The big joke we had with Allie was that she'd "upgraded" when she'd changed schools this year, after her parents had divorced and her mom moved to the next town over. Vista Green had a brand-new building, with state-of-the-art classrooms and materials, and it even had super-yummy food.

A second later Tamiko's phone buzzed, and she held it so MacKenzie and I could read it. There was a photo with a delicious-looking plate of food on it, and the caption: Eggplant rotini and fresh green salad. Wanna trade?

I grabbed the phone and texted back: This is Sierra. I love you, Allie, but I'd trade YOU for that lunch!

Allie responded with a string of emojis and a selfie of her taking a big bite of the rotini.

"I miss her," I said wistfully. Even though I still

23

had Tamiko, and MacKenzie was great, and I got to see Allie every Sunday, it wasn't the same as having her at school with me every day and living a bike ride away. Allie and I had spent so much time together in elementary school and sixth grade, and now we had to *schedule* time together. It just wasn't the same.

Tamiko nodded. "I miss her too," she said. "Allie is our glue! She keeps us all together. Right, Si?"

I hadn't really thought of it that way, but yes, Allie was kind of the mediator sometimes between Tamiko and me, since we occasionally butted heads because we were so different. MacKenzie was still a new enough friend that she didn't get involved.

Tamiko's phone buzzed again, and Tamiko quickly read the message out loud to us. "The weather's going to be really warm this weekend. You know what that means! Warm weather means everyone will want ice cream! Lots of customers at Molly's! Please be on time—early if you can make it!"

I said nothing but took a large forkful of mac and cheese. I knew what was coming.

"She means you," Tamiko said to me.

"I know," I replied. "Don't worry! I texted you last night—I made a really great schedule for myself for

24

the week, and I'm sticking to it. I will be everywhere I need to be, when I need to be there. I promise."

I made sure there was a smile in my voice when I said it, but even so, I caught MacKenzie throwing me another sympathetic glance. I was definitely going to have to watch myself with Tamiko for a few days. I may have been forgiven, but the episode hadn't been forgotten.

CHAPTER THREE
LEAD SINGER?

Thanks to all the careful planning I'd done Monday night, my week went by almost flawlessly. I managed to get to all of my sports practices, meetings, and lighting rehearsals, and completed all of my homework. My science test even seemed to go pretty well, although I bet Isa got a higher score because she went to that extra study session.

Feeling organized and on top of things for once, I glided into Molly's Ice Cream parlor on Sunday ready to enjoy a fun work shift with my friends. I'd missed Allie terribly all week and wanted to make sure I spent some extra time catching up with her.

Allie was already there behind the counter. She looked up when the bell tinkled and I walked in, and she flashed me an enormous smile. "Sierra! You're here!"

While I was glad to be so joyously welcomed, I couldn't help feeling slightly prickly inside. I was *always* there for my shift. Yes, I'd missed a few minutes here and there, but I'd never canceled or bailed on anyone.

"I'm here," I said quickly. "Where's Tamiko?"

Allie giggled. "You beat her here. But don't make a big deal out of it."

I laughed too. "Don't worry. I won't."

Allie and I refilled the toppings together and checked all the ice cream flavors to make sure none were low and needed to be replaced. While we worked, I filled her in how much fun I was having being the lighting director for the school play.

"I never would have pictured you as the lighting director," Allie said. "You're so sunny and bubbly! I would have thought you'd be onstage."

I shrugged. It was hard to explain how much I liked the precise work of following the script and knowing every lighting cue, and making sure the spotlight was always exactly where it needed to be, when it needed to be there. Maybe it was partly my math brain that enjoyed it.

Tamiko breezed in two minutes before one o'clock. She was wearing a terrific fringy crocheted vest that looked like she'd made it herself.

"Great vest, Tamiko!" I said, hoping to keep the conversation off my punctuality and on more interesting things . . . like hanging out together.

"Thanks!" she said, beaming. "I've been working on it for days. My aunt gave me some yarn and a pattern book, and I watched a bunch of crochet how-to videos online, then gave it a try."

"If it's not too hard, will you make me one?" I asked.

"Sure!" she said. "You know I love to spread my style around."

The three of us joked around a bit together, and Allie put on some upbeat music. A few of our nicest regular customers came in—a family with twin boys who always ordered one of Tamiko's custom concoctions, the It Takes Two sundae; and an older couple who liked to try something new every time they came.

We were having such a good time, it was like the previous weekend had never happened. I smiled at everyone who came in. Even my math calculations

(I always tried to add up the orders and make change in my head, even though the register did it for me) came quickly and easy.

After a while Mrs. Shear came out front and was pleased to see several happy customers sitting at tables inside and outside Molly's on this unusually warm day enjoying their ice cream. There was no line, so she pulled us all together behind the counter to talk.

"Girls, I have some good news," she said. "Business has been great lately, and a huge part of that is because of you three! So I had an idea for something nice I can do for you. I'm going to start an Employee of the Month program. Each month I'll choose one of you girls or one of our two college employees, the person who has gone above and beyond the call of duty, and I'll give you a little something extra. Maybe cash, maybe a day off, or maybe a little prize—I haven't decided yet."

Allie, Tamiko, and I looked at one another and spontaneously hugged. This was the best news ever!

"Thank you, Mrs. S.!" Tamiko gushed. "This is such a great idea. It will bring out the best in all of us. I know it."

Mrs. Shear grinned. "Well, I think you already

give your best, but I'll take it. Now I'm heading back-stage again, but holler if you need me."

Allie, Tamiko, and I did a little happy dance together, discussing what else being employee of the month might include. A picture of the employee on the wall? A special ice cream flavor named after the employee?

We were chatting so much that I hardly noticed when a bunch of customers came in all at once.

Tamiko snapped to attention to take their orders, and I began adding the items up in my head, not letting myself use the register. As I calculated, I hummed, because it helped me concentrate.

I must have been humming more loudly than usual because I saw Tamiko and Allie exchange an amused look.

"Sierra is our little songbird," Tamiko explained to our customers. "Luckily, she has a nice voice, or it might get on our nerves, because she hums and sings *all the time*."

Tamiko rolled her eyes when she said it, but in a good-natured way that let me know she really did like my humming.

I tugged on her apron playfully. "You're just jeal-

ous that you can't sing as well as IIIIII can, la, la, la!"
I sang to her.

A girl who was waiting for a Rockin' Rocky
Road double scoop studied me. "You really do have a
nice voice," she said. The girl had red hair and freckles,
which looked cool and chic. Her red hair was slicked
up into a tight, high ponytail, and she wore shiny
clear lip gloss. "Do you sing?"

I wasn't sure how to answer that. Wasn't it obvious
that I sang? I mean, I was just doing it.

The girl must have sensed my confusion, because
she added, "I mean, do you *really* sing, like in a choir
or a band, or take voice lessons?"

"Oh," I said. "Um, well, no. I mean, I sing all the
time, when I'm working, or in the shower, or doing
homework. And I hum when I take tests, which drives
people nuts, but I'm not in a choir or anything."

"She's in the school play," Allie interjected,
sounding like she was defending me, even though
there was no need to. The girl had just asked a question.

I laughed and whacked Allie on the shoulder.
"You goof," I said. "I'm the lighting director. Not one
of the stars."

The red-haired girl laughed and said, "It's not a trick question or anything. I'm asking because I'm in an all-girl band, and we're looking for a lead singer. I like your voice a lot. Would you come and audition for us?"

I couldn't believe what I was hearing. Someone wanted me to sing for real? For their *band*?

"Lead singer? Me?" I asked incredulously. "You can't be serious."

Tamiko elbowed me sharply in the ribs to let me know I was not being a very cool cucumber about the whole thing. "What's the name of the band?" she asked, to give me a minute to compose myself.

"The Wildflowers," the girl said. "I'm Reagan, by the way, and I play the drums."

"I like your band name," said Tamiko. "How'd you come up with it?"

Reagan looked thoughtful for a moment. "You know, I can't really remember! No special reason. It's not like we're actually *wild* or anything. We just liked how it sounded."

I laughed as I handed her the change. "I'm Sierra," I said, my mind still reeling from the mention of the word "audition."

"It's nice to meet you, Sierra. What do you think? Are you interested?"

I hesitated, and not because I wasn't interested. I most definitely *was*. I just felt put on the spot and needed a minute to process things. "Can I think about it, Reagan? It's not something I've ever even considered before!"

"And Sierra's involved in a lot of other activities already," Tamiko chimed in, looking pointedly at me.

I felt a stone drop in my stomach. Tamiko was right. I had made it through this past week, but only by being way more organized than I wanted to be.

Reagan nodded. "I get it," she said. She grabbed a napkin and wrote something on it. "Here's my number. If you decide you're interested, send me a text, okay? Don't even think of it as an audition. Just think of it as coming to sing and jam with a few friends. We're all really low-key. I promise."

"Okay. I'll think about it," I said. Then I quickly grabbed a spoonful of sprinkles and dusted the top of her cone with them. "Here—you can't leave without your little sprinkle of happy," I said, which was a customer tradition Allie and Tamiko and I had started.

33

Reagan took a bite. "Yum. *Very* happy. Nice to meet you! I hope I hear from you, Sierra."

And just like that, she was gone. I turned to look at my friends. Allie, who had been uncharacteristically silent throughout the conversation, had her jaw hanging open.

"Sierra! The lead singer in a band? I think you just got discovered," she said, grabbing my hands and holding them as she jumped up and down. "Can you believe this?"

I was pleased that Allie was so happy, but I didn't even know how *I* felt about it yet. Plus, I was slightly embarrassed at being singled out for something I'd done without meaning to. "Not so fast, Allie. I don't even know if I want to try out."

But even as I said the words, I was already picturing it in my mind: *The Wildflowers—starring lead singer Sierra Perez!*

"Sierra, you *have* to try out. You just have to. I'll go with you if you want," Allie offered.

I looked at Tamiko, who'd been so cheerful and fun, like her old self, all afternoon. Now there was a slight frown on her face. "It *is* really cool, Sierra," she said. "And you do have a great voice. But do you really have room in your life for one more thing? Remember your promise to Molly's!"

I did remember my promise: I wouldn't add anything more to my plate. And I'd also just had the best work day ever with my two best friends.

I would have to think very, very carefully.

CHAPTER FOUR
SISTERLY ADVICE

At home in my bedroom that night, I sat once again with my planner, looking at my upcoming week and making sure I was slotting in enough time for homework, projects, and my other commitments. Each day of the week was jam-packed with notes and scribbles and reminders of things I had to do and where I had to be. But when I asked myself *What could I cut out?* the answer was always *Nothing*. Because I loved each and every activity and had so much fun doing them!

Actually, that wasn't entirely true. I didn't particularly enjoy studying or homework, but those weren't optional. And I didn't enjoy being this organized either—I liked to go with the flow. But I couldn't afford another slip-up. I needed to be responsible.

I needed someone to talk to about the Wild-flowers audition, and I didn't feel comfortable texting Allie or Tamiko, because even though they seemed supportive at Molly's, I was afraid they'd turn it into a discussion about my chronic late-ness. And I didn't want to tell my parents yet either, because then my mom would bring up the play and get that worried look on her face where she got two huge creases between her eyebrows. There was one other option, though. Someone who might under-stand the allure of auditioning for a band and doing something different.

Before I could think twice, I was knocking on my sister's bedroom door, which for the past few months had remained closed to the family twenty-four hours a day. Isa even cleaned her room herself each week, dragging the vacuum, the duster, and clean sheets up there, just so our parents would agree to stay out. Recently Isa had hidden a pet snake in the room, so she'd had good reason to be so private, but since she'd given the snake away and she and I had each adopted a kitten, I wondered why the door remained shut. Was it a signal to me?

Knock, knock.

"Who's there?" Isa called, sounding mildly annoyed.

I wanted to start one of our old favorite knock-knock jokes from when we were little, like, *Orange. Orange who? Orange you glad I didn't say "Banana"?* But I wasn't sure Isa would laugh.

So instead I said, "It's me."

"Well, come in, ME," Isa replied.

I opened the door cautiously, wondering what I'd find in Isa's sanctum. It was as neat as a pin, like the last time I'd been in there. Her room stood in sharp contrast to the rest of our house, which was pleasantly messy, including my room.

Isa was lying on her bed reading a graphic novel, while her kitten, Cinnamon, kept swatting at her hair, vying for her attention. I was a little jealous. Cinnamon adored Isa and was always in her face, while my kitten, Marshmallow, was independent and liked to prowl the house looking for action.

Without lifting her eyes from her book, Isa asked, "What is it? I'm kind of busy."

Normally I might just give up on talking to Isa, because sometimes she deliberately tried to exhaust me, but this was too important. "I need help, Isa. Can you stop reading and playing with Cinnamon for a couple of minutes and talk to me?"

"I guess." With a sigh Isa shut her book and sat up, pulling Cinnamon into her lap. "What's up?"

I sat down on the end of her bed. I paused dramatically for a moment, because I knew that Isa enjoyed being a little dramatic herself.

"Have you ever thought about performing?" I asked her.

That got her attention. Isa's eyebrows shot up, and suddenly she leaned forward toward me and was ready to chat. "Performing? What do you mean, like being an actress?"

"Not an actress—a singer. A *lead* singer. In a band!" I said. Now that I had her complete attention, I explained the situation and how I'd met Reagan at Molly's. And for once Isabel looked impressed.

"Wow—that *is* cool," she said. "I don't think *I* could ever perform in front of people. But you do love to sing! How often would you rehearse? And what about soccer and softball and all that?"

Saying the words "I might audition for a band"

and seeing how impressed Isa had been had reinforced for me exactly how awesome this opportunity was. "Why does everyone keep harping on my schedule all the time?" I grumbled. "You sound like Allie and Tamiko."

Isa frowned. "You mean Allie and Tamiko aren't excited for you? They know you love to sing."

"No, they're excited. It's just . . . well, lately they've been on my case about being late for work a few times."

It was strange to be bonding and talking openly with Isa about my best friends not being support-ive, instead of talking to my friends about my sister ignoring me. It was like *Freaky Friday* or something. It reminded me of when we were little and Isa had been my best friend in the whole world.

I realized suddenly how much I missed that.

"Well, you can't stop being yourself because of your friends," Isa said, her voice growing slightly bitter. "Do what feels good and right to *you*, and if they don't like it, then they aren't your friends. Find new friends."

"Whoa," I said, holding up my hands. Isa was tak-ing my comment further than I'd meant it. "That's not it—they're still my best friends. They're just concerned." I was surprised by Isa's tone. Had something happened with one of her own friends? "Is everything okay with you?" I asked her.

"Yes, Sunshine," she said. "I'm just fine. I'm being *myself*. Which is what I think you should do too. You love to sing. Try out—see what happens. It's your life, not yours and Allie's and Tamiko's."

I let that sink in. She was right—it was my choice. And I did love to sing. And hadn't I handled everything my busy life had thrown at me up till now? I mean, a few minutes late here and there wasn't so terrible.

"I think your biggest problem is going to be Mom and Dad worrying about your grades," Isa added.

"My grades are fine," I said dismissively, with a wave of my hand. "And anyway, Mom always says she loves my singing. And performing is all about building confidence, right? Mom loves that stuff."

"Then what's stopping you from auditioning?" Isa smirked. She flopped back against her pillows and opened her book again. Cinnamon yowled with displeasure about no longer being in Isa's lap.

"Can you shut my door on your way out?"

Feeling like I'd just had the best talk with Isa that I'd had in a very long time, I hopped up and patted her foot awkwardly. "Sure, Isa. And thanks."

Back in my room I found Reagan's number and punched it into my phone, then sent her a text that I'd love to audition for her band. Then I found her on SuperSnap and followed her.

A few minutes later, as I was starting my social studies homework, I got a notification that she'd followed me back on SuperSnap and had sent me a message.

Can't wait for ur audition, Sierra!

Then she sent a second message: What does ur SuperSnap account name mean?

My SuperSnap account was "sisip3," so I got that question a lot. Sisi is a nickname that my family calls me. P stands for my last name, Perez. 3 is my lucky number!

Gotcha! Reagan replied. Perez is easy to remember because both of my vets are named Dr. Perez!

Reagan knew my parents? That was even better! Now Mom and Dad would be more comfortable with me joining the band.

The Perez doctors are my parents! I texted back. Who's your pet?

That's so cool! I have a rabbit named Thistle, and they helped us so much when she was sick last year. See you on Saturday at noon for your audition! ☺

Just then my dad walked by my bedroom and saw me sitting and texting on my phone, while surrounded by a pile of textbooks.

"Sierra," he said warningly. It was a no-no in our house to use your phone while doing homework, even though it actually helped sometimes to be able to text a classmate a question. Still, I knew the rules.

"Sorry, Papi," I said, putting the phone down quickly. "It's just that I met someone named Reagan Leone at Molly's today, and she says you treated her bunny rabbit."

To my surprise Dad laughed. "Oh yes—the Leones' rabbit. That poor bunny is pretty old. They're a nice family. They live not far from here." Dad peered at my books, as if trying to decide how much more homework I had left by how tall the stack was.

"I'll be done soon," I said. "And no phone until then, I promise."

"Okay," he said. "Sweet dreams, Sierra."

As I dove back into my homework, I couldn't help thinking it had to be a sign that my parents knew Reagan. It wasn't just a coincidence, right? This meant that I *had* to audition for the Wildflowers!

CHAPTER FIVE
ROCK STAR!

Telling my parents about the audition had gone better than I'd expected. Isa had been right—Mom had been so excited about me doing something involving singing that she'd forgotten to freak out about my schedule, and since Dad already knew and liked Reagan's family, he'd even offered to drive me to the audition.

Tamiko had asked me at school the day before whether I was going to audition or not, and I'd told her I was still thinking about it, which was sort of a lie. But since I knew I'd see her the next day at our work shift, I decided I would only mention it to her and Allie if I actually got in to the band. Because if I *didn't* get in, I'd have to tell them the bad news. So really I was making everyone's lives easier by keeping it to myself, right?

Dad dropped me off at the Leones' house at exactly noon.

"Call me when you're ready to be picked up, rock star," he joked.

I grinned back at him, even as the butterflies in my stomach began whirling. "Thank you, Papi!" I said. "Love you."

I made sure to knock firmly on Reagan's door, as if I weren't nervous and I did things like this all the time. Reagan answered a moment later, looking cool and sleek again. This time her dark red hair was carefully smoothed into a long side braid, and she had three clip-on hoops climbing up her left ear.

"Hey, Sierra!" she said. "I'm so glad you're here. The other girls are really excited to meet you."

She led me through the house and out a side door to the driveway. "We practice in the garage," she explained. "It keeps my mom happy—even though she swears she thinks we're pretty good. She still doesn't want us practicing in the house. And I guess I don't blame her. Anyway, here we are! Everybody, this is Sierra."

I stepped into the garage, which had the usual shelves full of tools, bike helmets, and camping equipment but also had a rug in the middle with a drum set, a keyboard, a few amps, and some music stands positioned on it.

Seated behind the keyboard was a girl wearing a Decemberists T-shirt and washed-out black jeans. She had a short Afro, and the tips of her hair were dyed blond. "Hey. I'm Kasey," she said. Her dark eyes sparkled, and she gave me a big smile. "I can't wait to hear you sing."

"Thanks," I said. "I, uh, can't wait to hear you play."

"And I'm Tessa," said a girl with long, dirty-blond hair. "I play guitar and write most of our original songs. I love to sing, but my voice isn't strong enough to solo, so that's why we've been talking about adding a real lead singer."

A *real* lead singer? Me? I was starting to wonder if I was cool enough to be in this band. They wrote their own music, and they had an awesome garage to practice in. And they all looked super-passionate about music. I wanted to ask them a thousand questions about how long they'd been playing their instruments, and when they'd started the band, and if they ever played for people, but I needed to focus on my audition and on singing my heart out. I already knew I wanted to be a part of this group, and singing well was my way in.

Reagan took her place behind the drum set and picked up her sticks. She tapped them together three times and said in a loud announcer's voice, "And I'm Reagan on the drums. Welcome to the Wildflowers!"

She banged on the drums dramatically. Everyone laughed, and some of my nerves disappeared. These girls were fun. They were going to be nice about it, even if I stank.

Reagan turned to Tessa. "Tessa, why don't you hand Sierra the lyrics to that new song you wrote? We'll play it a few times first so that she can get the melody."

Tessa nodded and handed me a sheet of paper. At the top of the page was written "'You're the One,' by Tessa Villes," and then the lyrics followed.

> *You're the one.*
> *I see you in my dreams.*
> *You're the one.*

But telling you is harder than it seems.
You're the one.
My love is deep and true!
You're the one.
But what if I'm not . . . not the one for you?

The girls started playing, with Kasey and Reagan watching Tessa on guitar so that they could stay together. I listened to the music and sang the lyrics softly to myself to try to get the melody right. The song was catchy and not particularly hard to learn. Still, it wasn't easy to come in cold and sing a song I'd never heard before! I'd prepared a song called "Always Together" that was really popular at the moment. I'd had no idea that I'd be asked to sing an original two minutes after hearing it!

"Well, what do you think?" Reagan asked anxiously.

I couldn't believe Reagan was even asking. They were so good! "I really liked it," I said. "It's catchy, but it's also a little sad. Like all the best songs, right?"

"Exactly!" said Kasey. "Tessa wrote it about her crush."

I glanced over at Tessa, whose face had turned a

bright pink, and she was looking down at the floor. "Thanks a heap, *Kasey*," she said. "Tell everyone, why don't you?"

"Don't be embarrassed," I said quickly. "We've all had crushes! They can be really fun. And then sometimes, maybe not so fun. But without them we wouldn't have many good songs, would we?"

Tessa nodded, still looking slightly embarrassed. But then she looked up and met my eyes, giving me a grateful smile. "Thanks, Sierra."

"Do you think you could try singing it?" Reagan asked excitedly. "We haven't heard anyone sing it solo yet. Just the three of us harmonizing."

I nodded. "It might take me a few tries to get it right, but let's do it."

"Woo-hoo! Okay, Wildflowers . . . let's hit it," Reagan said. She tapped her drumsticks together a few times, saying, "A one, a two, a one, two, three, four!"

The girls began playing, and I followed along with the music, waiting for my cue.

Then I took a deep breath and sang the lyrics, careful to stay in tempo with the girls.

When I was done, I looked at the girls, waiting for their reactions. I thought it had sounded pretty good, but I wasn't sure what they were looking for in a singer. Maybe I hadn't been strong enough.

"That was great!" Reagan said. She turned to Kasey. "What did you think?"

Kasey beamed at me. "It was *really* great," she said. "You have a beautiful voice, Sierra."

"Tessa?" Reagan said. "What did you think?"

Tessa's eyes were shining. "It sounded even better than I'd imagined it. Thank you, Sierra. They're my words, but you sang them with so much feeling!"

I felt myself blushing. I'd had so much fun singing the song, but I knew I could do better, and I told them so. "So can we try it again, please?"

"Of course," said Reagan slowly, looking around at Kasey and Tessa carefully, as if measuring something. "In fact, we'll probably be doing it *many* times, because guess what? We'd love to have you join the Wildflowers! That is, if you're still interested."

My mouth dropped open. "That was the whole audition? I had a song prepared for you guys and everything!" I said.

Kasey shrugged. "So sing it! We've got all afternoon. Let's jam out and have some fun. You're a yes, right?"

"Um, of *course* I am!" I said. "Until I met Reagan, I'd never even thought about joining a band. But then once she said something, I haven't been able to *stop* thinking about it for days!"

Reagan gave us a little drumroll and said, "And then there were four . . . ta-daaaa!" while the other girls cheered.

I couldn't remember the last time I'd been so happy. And I couldn't wait to tell Allie and Tamiko. I knew that as soon as I explained how much fun the band was, and what it felt like to stand up and sing with them, even if it was just in someone's garage, they would understand. It felt like fireworks going off in my body. It felt amazing.

We played and practiced for another two hours, working through some pop songs from the radio as well as some of the original songs Tessa had written. Sometimes we made mistakes and didn't listen to one another, and then we tried the song over and over until we got it. As we were getting ready to leave, the girls gave me a stack of music to start learning.

"I'll start tonight," I promised. I couldn't wait. I'd be singing in the shower, in the car, in math class. And probably at Molly's, too.

Now I had to tell Allie and Tamiko. I could wait and tell them in person the next day, but I didn't think I could keep it in for another twenty-four hours.

Dad picked me up, and the minute I got home, I took a selfie in my room, holding my hairbrush like a microphone. I captioned it, Sierra Perez, Official Rock Star and Lead Singer of the Wildflowers, and sent it to both of them.

Allie immediately texted back a bunch of happy-face emojis and hands clapping, and then wrote, Awesome! Knew you could do it! Tamiko texted back, Congrats! Remember us when ur rich and famous!

I exhaled with relief. It had actually happened—I had auditioned and been invited to join the Wildflowers. And what made it even sweeter was that my friends were excited about it with me.

It had been a perfect day.

CHAPTER SIX
COFFEE AND DOUGHNUTS
AND APOLOGIES

In the blink of an eye, two weeks went by. Two weeks of very careful scheduling, staying up late to get caught up on schoolwork, and juggling soccer and softball practices with making posters for student council, attending play rehearsals, and practicing with the Wildflowers. I couldn't believe how fast time was moving, and no matter what time of day it was, I was always somewhere doing something. I was both exhausted *and* happy, because I loved it all, and I was getting it all done.

But as they say, all good things must come to an end.

The school play was opening in just a few days, and I had to run the lights for one of the final dress rehearsals on Sunday morning. There was no one else who could do it—I was the lighting director. Besides, I'd been late to the last lighting run-through because I'd been at a softball game.

So when rehearsal ran a bit long and I knew I was going to be late for my shift at Molly's, I decided to stop off at Allie and Tamiko's favorite bakery and pick up some doughnuts for them. It was hard to be mad at someone with the smell of fresh doughnuts in the air, right?

I whooshed through the door of Molly's, wincing as the tinkling bell announced my lateness yet again. Did it *have* to be so loud?

Both Allie and Tamiko were serving customers, so they didn't stop to look at me or say anything. I quietly slid my box of doughnuts onto our side of the counter behind the ice cream containers, grabbed my apron, and headed to the cash register. This time I'd already pulled my hair back before I'd arrived.

As I made change for the last person in line, I wondered how things would go. I almost wished it would stay jammed in Molly's all afternoon, so that my friends and I wouldn't have to talk for a few hours. It might give them time to simmer down.

But the last person disappeared quickly, and when the three of us were all alone, I turned to face them. I knew I needed to just deal with it.

"I'm *very* sorry," I said. "It was the play! It's our last weekend of rehearsals before the show opens Friday. Then it'll be over and it'll be one huge thing off my plate." I smiled, hoping they'd agree that that was good news.

But Allie and Tamiko were both stone-faced, busying themselves by doing some unnecessary cleaning and not meeting my eyes.

"I brought you doughnuts," I tried in a singsongy voice, picking up the box and waving it under their noses. "Because I know it was wrong for me not to be here. And of course I'll stay an extra twenty minutes. Or thirty, even, to make up for it. Okay, guys?"

But my friends weren't having it.

"What were you thinking?" Tamiko whispered. "The stupid doughnuts made you even *later*."

"Yeah," said Allie. "And this time my mom's here! And she's come out front twice looking for you."

Right then Mrs. Shear came out from backstage. She saw me holding the box of doughnuts and frowned.

"Sierra? What's going on?" she asked. Her normally cheerful face was pulled into a frown, and her eyes flicked to the clock on the wall. "Did you just get here?"

I froze like an ice cube. I couldn't stand being scolded by adults. Not by my own parents, not by teachers or coaches, not by anyone. I'd hated it ever since I was little and had forgotten to take the bathroom pass in first grade, and our teacher had yelled at me in front of the whole class.

I tried to think of something to say, but before I could find the words, Tamiko blurted out, "Sierra was late because she had an idea for a new ice cream flavor."

What?

I stared at Tamiko, not following her at all. The front door's bell tinkled again. Two older ladies walked in and strolled up to the ice cream display to browse.

Mrs. Shear's eyebrow relaxed somewhat. "Oh. Really?" she asked. "So what's the new flavor, Sierra?"

Oh no—new flavors and concoctions were not my strong suit. That was Tamiko's specialty! I looked from the customers to Mrs. Shear and gulped, my

57

mind a total blank. I was about to blurt out "jelly doughnut" and pray that Mrs. Shear laughed, or at least smiled, when Tamiko saved me yet again.

"Sierra's so modest," Tamiko said, laughing. "It's Coffee and Doughnuts. Sort of like an afternoon pick-me-up—coffee ice cream with bits of fresh doughnut mixed in."

With perfect timing, almost as if we were in a play, the two older ladies who'd been browsing the ice cream flavors immediately spoke up.

"Um, excuse us," one lady said, "but we couldn't help overhearing.... Do you have Coffee and Dough-nuts ice cream? That sounds *delicious*."

Tamiko beamed proudly, apparently forgetting that she'd just given *me* credit for the idea. She looked at Mrs. Shear, waiting to see if she'd approve the new flavor.

"Well," Mrs. Shear replied, looking doubtful, "we could. I mean, we might *soon*. But all the ingredients here at Molly's are homemade, and that includes the mix-ins, except for sprinkles and things, and I haven't *made* these doughnuts. They're store-bought—"

"Oh, that's no problem!" said the lady. "We won't tell. Couldn't we just be taste testers? And then if it works out, you could add it to the menu, right?"

I felt like I was watching a court case with my own fate being decided. If the flavor worked out and the ladies liked it, I had a feeling I wouldn't be in much trouble. But if it *didn't* work out, then I was done for.

"We've just come from book club," said the other woman. "And the book was a real downer this month. We need a pick-me-up!"

Mrs. Shear's face broke into a smile. "Well, then, of course. Just this once, though, and it's on the house. Then it'll be homemade doughnuts in our Coffee and Doughnuts flavor. Okay?"

"Coming right up!" Tamiko said cheerfully, handing the box of doughnuts to Allie.

Allie smiled back and quickly began chopping up a chocolate doughnut into tiny bits and adding them to a cup of coffee ice cream. I had to admit, it looked delicious. Tamiko was something of a genius.

The two ladies each took a taste and couldn't stop complimenting us. Mrs. Shear was so pleased by all the praise, I thought her head was going to fly off her body.

"Don't thank me," said Mrs. Shear. "Thank this

wonderful girl here for coming up with it." She wrapped an arm around me and squeezed.

Tamiko glanced at me, and I felt like a *jerk*. I was so grateful not to be in trouble, and yet at the same time I felt *so bad* because I was getting credit for something I really didn't deserve.

The two ladies oohed and aahed over their specials some more and then left, leaving behind a generous tip in the tip jar.

Mrs. Shear studied me thoughtfully. "Well, Sierra, I guess I owe you an apology. I was about to scold you for being late, when really you were working hard and thinking up a great new idea for Molly's! In the future, though, I'd prefer that you check with me first before you go off and do any shopping for the store."

"Yes, of course, Mrs. Shear," I said meekly.

Mrs. Shear patted me lightly on the shoulder. "I'll be in the back finishing up some paperwork," she said. "But—Coffee and Doughnuts! I love it. Good work. We need more great ideas like this from you!"

As soon as she was out of earshot, I walked to the tip jar and pulled out the money the ladies had left. "Here, Tamiko. This should be yours for saving my behind. And you too, Allie, for not telling on me to your mom. I'm so embarrassed. You guys totally saved me, and now I'm stuck taking credit for your good idea! That's not what I wanted."

Tamiko took her half of the money and put it into her pocket. "You owe us BIG-TIME, Sierra," she said. "You made a promise that you wouldn't add one more thing to your schedule. And then you joined the Wildflowers. And Allie and I were *super*cool about it, and we've been so supportive, because we understand what an amazing opportunity this is. But if you can't fit in Molly's, too, then maybe you should think about quitting and letting us hire someone who actually shows up on time."

I couldn't believe what I was hearing.

"Hire someone else?" I squeaked. "But this is our special time together! The Sprinkle Squad! The Sprinkle Sundays sisters! We can't lose that."

Allie looked sad as she handed me a box of cones to unpack and stack. "Maybe we've already lost it. Those are just words, Sierra, if you can't make it here to be with us. Right?"

She was right. Unless I showed them that they were a priority like my other activities, they had every right to think about replacing me. I wondered who they would ask. MacKenzie? One of Allie's new friends from Vista Green? It was a horrible thought.

The idea that I might be replaceable gave me a terrible ache in my stomach. I'd been telling myself that I wasn't as *needed* here at Molly's as I was at some of my other activities, because there were two people to cover for me until I arrived. But maybe what mattered more was that I was *wanted*. I was wanted by my two best friends, and I was leaving them hanging.

CHAPTER SEVEN
TESSA'S CRUSH REVEALED

Even though I managed to make it to all of my commitments over the next few days, including a spur-of-the-moment student council meeting (which luckily ended up being at lunch and not after school), softball practice, and a play rehearsal, I wasn't the usual Sierra. I felt guilty and selfish, because my friends were right—I had prioritized certain activities over them. I hadn't done it consciously, but I'd done it. So even though my careful scheduling was mostly working, because I was pretty much getting everything done without my grades suffering, my friendships weren't working.

On Thursday, I was getting ready to head over to an evening practice with the Wildflowers at Reagan's house. They'd moved it from early afternoon to accommodate my schedule, which I definitely felt bad about, considering I was a brand-new member, but it was better than not practicing.

I loved being part of the band. It was a lot of work, though, because in addition to the rehearsals, I had to learn all the words to Tessa's songs, as well as some pop hits we'd been practicing.

I stood in the kitchen, packing my bag with sheet music. I hummed to myself, trying out a new harmony that might work for Tessa's song "Don't Stay a Stranger."

Isa was in the kitchen too, rooting around in the fridge for a snack. She turned to look at me and pretended to hold up a remote control and hit the mute button. I just sang louder.

"Do you ever stop?" she asked.

"Nope—I'm a singing machine!"

Isa rolled her eyes as my dad came into the kitchen to grab his keys.

"Papi," she said in an uncharacteristically sweet voice, "after you drop off Sierra, would you take me to Molly's? I've been looking for a snack, and I suddenly realized that what I really want is ice cream, and we don't have any."

Dad looked pleased. Isa didn't often ask anyone to take her anywhere. She usually went off with her group of friends on her skateboard.

"*Sí, sí,* of course," he said. "Sierra, do you want to come with us? I could drop you at practice after. Your mom could come too. We haven't all gone out for ice cream in ages."

For a second I considered it. I'd have loved to stop by Molly's on a weeknight and see Allie. I never got to see her during the week anymore! Sometimes she and Tamiko met up together at the mall or at each other's houses, but I had too many activities and could never make it.

It was also pretty rare to have Isa *willing* to hang out with us as a family. In public, no less.

But I couldn't be late for my practice—not after they'd moved it for me. That would be terrible. So I said, "Thanks, Papi, but I really need to be on time. Bring me home a cup of Lemon and Lime?"

Dad winked at me. "Of course. Let's go, girls! I'm getting myself a giant sundae tonight. I deserve a treat. I had to clean out a pig's infected ears today. You don't want to know what that's like."

Practice was great. I tested out some of the harmonies I'd been working on, and the other girls loved them. Kasey had a great voice for harmonizing and wasn't as shy about singing as Tessa was. Reagan would sometimes sing along as well but mostly preferred to just play drums. But when the four of us did all sing together, it sounded really good.

After about an hour we took a break. Reagan went inside and grabbed a pitcher of lemonade she'd made earlier and some chips and salsa, and we all sat around and talked for a bit. Reagan's garage had an old sofa on one side, and she'd hung up some twinkle lights along the ceiling so that it didn't feel quite so garage-y at night.

After she'd finished eating, Reagan stood up and clapped her hands. "Wildflowers, I have a big announcement. I've been waiting to tell you until now because I wanted to make sure we were *really* ready, and I think we are."

Tessa sucked in her breath. "Holy cow, seriously?"

I turned to look at her. "'Holy cow, seriously' what? Do you already know what she's going to say?"

Kasey's eyes were open wide, and she nodded at me. "Yes. Don't you?"

I didn't. I had no idea.

Reagan jumped up and down a few times, like an excited kindergartner going out for recess. "My cousin wants us to play at his birthday party next Saturday!" she announced.

There was a moment of silence, and then a collective shriek as we all jumped up and started hugging one another.

Suddenly we all stopped jumping and stood and stared at one another. It was exciting news, for sure, but also a bit nerve-racking.

I wondered if I should even say the next words. "Um, are we ready for this?" I asked. Was that breaking some sort of band code? Were we supposed to believe in ourselves 100 percent, all the time? Wasn't there some "fake it till you make it" saying in show business? "I mean, will we really be ready to perform . . . *in front of people* . . . by next Saturday?"

Reagan laughed. "Is anyone ever ready?" she said. "I don't know. But he wants us there. He said, at least this way he's guaranteed four fun, super-awesome people at his party. We'll have to make time for some extra practice, though. Right, girls?"

All of us nodded, me nodding the hardest, while mentally scanning my schedule in my head. The play would be over this weekend, but I had softball games, a soccer game, tests, Molly's . . . and now a real gig that required extra practices! I didn't see how I could possibly do it all. On the other hand, how could I possibly *not*? I couldn't let down my bandmates. Or teammates. Or thespian-mates.

"Sierra, your friend Allie might know my cousin," Reagan said, interrupting my thoughts. "His name is Patrick Ryan, and he's at Vista Green too."

"Oh, ummm, I don't think she's ever mentioned him, but I'll ask her," I said. I picked up my glass of lemonade and took a sip, unable to stop worrying about the extra rehearsals and Molly's.

"So, Tessa, do you think your crush might be at the party?" Kasey asked in a teasing voice. "He goes to Vista Green too, right?"

Immediately poor Tessa flushed a bright pink. "Yeah, but I don't know if he knows Patrick," she said. "It's a big school, isn't it?"

Tessa sounded trembly at the mere mention of her crush. She wrote beautiful songs about him but was too shy to sing them herself, even in front of just us. I couldn't imagine her ever directly telling anyone she liked him.

I smiled at her encouragingly. "I didn't know your crush went to Vista Green. What's his name? I mean, if you don't mind me asking."

Still blushing, Tessa said, "It's okay. His name is Colin Preston. Do you think your friend Allie knows him?"

I wanted to close my eyes and cringe, but I couldn't do that with all three girls staring at me. *Colin!*

There couldn't be two Colin Meehans at Vista Green. Which meant that Tessa's crush just happened to be the same boy that Allie had become really good friends with this year. And even though Allie always told Tamiko and me that she and Colin were just friends, Tamiko and I secretly thought maybe they liked each other and didn't want to admit it. Or at least Allie didn't. She'd had so much going on with her parents' divorce this year, and moving, and helping out at her mom's store—how could she have time for a crush, too?

I also had the feeling that even if Allie didn't like Colin *that way*, she'd still be kind of unhappy to know about Tessa's crush. Colin was one of her few good friends at her new school. He was one of the first people who'd been really nice to her and welcomed her there.

Kasey nudged me. "Sierra—are you in there? Does your friend Allie know Crushworthy Colin?"

"I have no idea," I fibbed. "I can ask her."

"No, don't," Tessa begged.

"I think my cousin Patrick knows him, though." Reagan's eyes lit up. "Oh, Tessa, I have an idea! Patrick can invite him, and then Sierra can sing your song at the party and dedicate it to Colin, and tell him it's from a secret admirer."

Tessa looked as if she were about to keel over. Kasey and Reagan both squealed, and I played along as if I thought it were a good idea, but in reality I would never, ever do that to Tessa. And anyway, what would Allie think? Allie had been so supportive of my being in the band, and had even kept me out of trouble with her mom when I was late, and now I was being asked to try to set up another girl with a boy she maybe secretly liked? I couldn't.

Reagan giggled at poor Tessa's stricken face. "Oh, we're just kidding, Tessa. We wouldn't do that. But, Sierra, you should invite Allie, since she's new to Vista

Green. My cousin won't mind, and I'm sure she'd like to hear us play, right?"

"Um, sure," I said, feeling not at *all* sure. Yes, it would be good for my friends to meet the band, but what if Colin were there? And then he and Allie ended up talking during the whole party and Tessa was heartbroken? Or the *reverse* happened? It was too much to worry about. But I couldn't tell the band that. So I said, "I'll invite her and our friend Tamiko. They'll cheer really loudly for us."

At least if both Allie and Tamiko came, Allie would spend most of the time with her. Then maybe the Colin thing wouldn't be a problem. Maybe it would also help them feel more included in my new rock-star life.

Kasey held up her hands and hooted. "That's two fans already! Plus Patrick. Pretty soon everyone will be wearing Wildflowers T-shirts and we'll get mobbed on the streets."

We all laughed and then got back up to practice some more, and I resolved not to worry too much about other people's love lives. With a real, actual gig coming up, we needed to focus. *I* needed to focus!

And I, for the next few weeks at least, had to find time to fit in even more practices, *and* find a way to show Allie and Tamiko that they were still my priority.

Friends first. Music second. That was doable, right?

CHAPTER EIGHT
CRUSHWORTHY COLIN

The Wildflowers and I managed to practice again really early Saturday morning, before my softball game, and then again on Sunday morning. I couldn't make it any days after school in the upcoming week, so that was the best I could do. No one liked the early morning practices, but I'd had the two showings of the school play on Friday and Saturday night, and both had gone great, so I was feeling pretty good about having one less thing to juggle as Dad picked me up from band rehearsal Sunday morning.

Not only that, but I had a full, unscheduled *hour* to myself before I had to head over to Molly's to work. It had been ages since I'd had any free time. When I wasn't actually engaged in any of my activities, I used every spare minute for studying, reading for English class (we were reading *My Ántonia*, and I kept having to read passages over and over again, so it made for slow going), or scheduling and moving practices and things around so that I could get everywhere on time. I'd noticed that my teammates and student council associates seemed to be getting pretty tired of my texts, no matter how many smiley emojis I used.

Oh well. I was doing my best. Now, about my one free hour. I was wondering: Should I use it to nap? Eat a leisurely lunch? Catch up on some reality TV?

Dad dropped me off at home, saying he was heading into the office to meet Mom. On Sundays they usually caught up on paperwork they didn't have time for during the week.

But as I walked into the house and deposited my bag of sheet music, I found Isa sitting at the kitchen counter, sipping a lemonade and looking as morose as I'd ever seen her. Cinnamon was winding herself around the legs of Isa's stool, yowling and looking annoyed because she wasn't in Isa's lap.

"Isa, what is it?" I asked.

Isa flashed her eyes at me but didn't answer. Instead

she went back to staring into her lemonade.

"*Isa*," I said. "You can talk to me, you know. I'm still your sister. And your twin."

Isa sighed. "There's nothing *twin* about us, Sunshine. You're you, and I'm me, and that's that."

Isa was great at deflecting questions and talking without actually saying anything. She did it to our parents all the time. And when she had stopped hanging out with me and Allie and Tamiko a year or two before and had started wearing dark, moody clothing, and even when she'd started changing her habits and hobbies, she would never just directly *say* why it was that she felt she needed to go in such a different direction from me. Not that there was anything wrong with her direction. It was just a big detour from where she'd been.

And I had asked her, over and over, *What changed?* She would shrug or say something obtuse. My parents said we had to just let Isa be Isa, but sometimes it would be nice if she'd open up a little.

I mean, what was the point of being twins if we didn't talk to each other?

"Well, you get good grades, so I'm guessing this isn't about homework or a test," I said, trying to wiggle something out of her. "And Cinnamon is right under your feet looking very healthy, so it's not your cat. Mom and Dad are at work, so you have the house to yourself. The only thing I can think of is that it's a friend problem."

Isa snorted. "*You're* the one with the friend problems."

I shook my head. "Nope—not me. I've worked everything out with my friends." I paused, then added, "Mostly," thinking of the weird party coming up with Colin and Allie and Tessa, not to mention the extra band rehearsals I hadn't told Allie and Tamiko about. But today I was going to be on time to Molly's, and that would count for a lot.

"Well, la–di–da," Isa replied.

She could sound tough, but she couldn't fool me. Underneath our different clothes and different personalities, we had the same face and the same DNA. And I knew when Isa was unhappy. I could practically feel it vibrating under my skin. Wasn't there a word for that? Twin–tuition or something?

But I knew just standing there badgering her to talk to me wouldn't work. It would have to be something more clever. Something to get her to relax and open up and be the fun, funny person I knew she was underneath.

"Want to play Battleship with me?" I asked.

We'd played Battleship many times as kids, and it was a good game for twins, because the whole point was to try to guess where the other person had put their battleships. And because we'd played each other so many times, we knew each other's strategies.

Isa looked at me disgustedly, or pretended to. "Seriously? Battleship? Aren't we, like, way too old for that?"

"You sound scared of losing," I taunted her.

"You haven't beaten me at Battleship in years," scoffed Isa. "You're too nice. And you put your ships too close together."

"Prove it," I said.

Isa pretended to dismiss the idea, but I knew that if I pushed, she'd say yes. And I knew deep down that with whatever was wrong with her, she needed some sister time in order to feel better.

"I'm getting it now," I said. "Get ready."

"Oh, fine," said Isa. "Whatever. I'm going to beat you."

I smiled as I walked to the den, where we kept the

games. I still knew my twin. And I was prepared to play very badly if it would cheer her up.

Maybe "Sunshine" wasn't such a bad nickname for me after all.

We started playing, and Isa took control quickly, finding both my destroyer and my cruiser (because I deliberately put them next to each other). Then Isa glanced at the clock and said, "Aren't you supposed to be at work soon?"

"OH NO!" I yelled, jumping up. "I'm going to be late, and I wasn't even *doing* anything!"

Isa looked offended.

"You know what I mean—like late coming from a rehearsal or something."

"Yeah, yeah, whatever. Just go. Don't let Allie and Tamiko boss you around, though, okay? They're not your bosses."

"I don't," I said, bristling. "But Molly's is my job. I have to be there. It has nothing to do with them."

"Yeah, okay," she said. "Stop talking to me and go. You'll have to run."

I made it to Molly's on time, but just barely. Like, I had ten seconds to spare. I had run the entire way, so when I burst in through the door, I couldn't help yelling, "Made it!"

I felt both proud and slightly amazed by my on-time arrival. Thank goodness for all of my soccer practices, or I wouldn't have been in such good running shape! My activities really did pay off.

Then I realized I was red-faced and panting, and more than a little sweaty, which was not a good look. Especially since there was a family in there buying cones for everyone.

Thankfully, the family was a really nice one and started laughing. I guess I had looked pretty ridiculous running in like that and making a big scene. Then Allie and Tamiko laughed, and before I knew it, I was basking in the warm glow of hanging out with my two best friends. Whatever juggling I had to do, it was worth it.

When the nice family left, after making jokes about someone needing to buy me a bike or a pair of roller skates, Allie patted me on the back.

"Sierra," she said. "You don't need to kill yourself. We want you here on time, but we also want you alive!"

See? Everything's fine with my friends, I wanted

to tell Isa. I laughed and tried to take a couple of deep breaths to slow my heart rate down. Panting all through my shift probably wasn't going to work.

"I just really didn't want to be late again," I explained. "And I was playing Battleship with Isa, and we lost track of time—"

"You were *what*?" Tamiko cut in. "You and Isa were playing a board game? Do tell."

I shrugged. "There's nothing to tell. We were just hanging out together. It was really nice, actually. Like old times."

"Is something going on?" asked Allie.

It had been so long since the four of us had hung out together, I guess I understood why she'd ask that. And I did complain to Allie and Tamiko a lot about how Isa would keep her door shut and not talk to me. But I also felt protective of her. No matter what, we were blood.

"Nope. Just having some sister time."

Allie raised an eyebrow at me but didn't ask any more questions. As a distraction I offered to go into the back and bring out a fresh tub of coffee ice cream, which we'd been using up super-fast since the intro-duction of the Coffee and Doughnuts flavor.

When I came back, there were customers and it got busy again for a while. I got to play my favorite game of adding up the cost of the orders in my head instead of on the register. So almost our whole shift went by before I remembered I had something important to tell my BFFs. And I still wasn't sure of the best way to say it.

"So, girls—I have some *news*," I began.

Tamiko looked interested. "Oh? Is this about a boy?"

I couldn't hide my surprise. "A boy? No, no, no, no. I hardly have time to brush my *teeth*, let alone think about any of the boys at school. Why? Is there a boy *you* like?"

Tamiko shook her head. "No. I was just saying that because of the way you said 'news.' The only one of us with any kind of boy 'friend' is Allie."

"Me?" said Allie, her voice a high-pitched squeak. "You mean Colin? He's just a friend-friend. Not a *boy*friend. A friend-friend, who is a boy, but isn't a boyfriend."

"Mmmm-hmm," said Tamiko, in a way that let us both know she didn't believe a word Allie had said.

I didn't either. Just the way she'd said his name—

Colllllllin—all slowly had made it sound like she at least thought of him as a little bit more than a random boy who sits next to her on the bus. She liked him!

"Anyway," I said, wanting to both change the subject and get this news out as quickly as possible, since now I *really* wasn't so sure Allie would want to hear it. "I have news."

"Then tell us already!" said Tamiko.

I couldn't help beaming as I said, "The Wildflowers will be making their *premier performance* next Saturday night at Reagan's cousin Patrick Ryan's birthday party," I told them. "And you're both invited!"

Allie and Tamiko both let out a shout. Then Allie said, "Patrick Ryan? Wait . . . does he go to my school? I think he's in my math class."

"Yes!" I told her. "That's great that you know him. Is he nice?"

Allie nodded. "I think so. I don't know him very well. He answers questions and acts like a human most of the time."

"Sounds nice enough," said Tamiko, laughing. "I'd love to go to a Vista Green party! We can meet some of your friends, Allie."

"Well, I still don't know *that* many people, but I'd love to hear you sing, Sierra."

"Yes!" Tamiko said. "I know you'll be great, Si. *And* a party means an excuse for me to put a new outfit together."

I was so happy at how excited they were about the party and my band playing. I crossed my fingers under the counter for a minute, like I used to do when I was seven or eight. The next part was going to be tricky.

"Oh, and there's one more thing!" I said, trying to sound casual. "Allie, could you please find out if Colin is going? Reagan thinks he and Patrick are friends, but she isn't sure."

"O-kkkaaay," said Allie. "But why does she want to be *sure* if Colin is going? Does she know him?"

Tamiko looked suspicious as well. "Yeah, and why wouldn't she just ask her cousin if he'd invited Colin? That would be easier."

Oh jeez. Now this whole thing *was* really awkward, because Tamiko had a great point. "Um, well, it's because she doesn't want to embarrass Tessa," I admitted. "Our guitar player and songwriter. She has . . . Well, she has a crush on Colin, and she's kind of hoping to see him there."

Allie kept her face blank as she answered, "Oh, I see. Okay."

Tamiko and I watched her, both of us wondering how she was feeling.

"That's not a problem, is it?" I asked. I was trying to play it cool, but I worried that maybe I had upset Allie. "You always say you guys are just friends, and I doubt Tessa would ever even *talk* to him because she's so shy. . . ."

I felt like I was blathering. Meanwhile, Allie's face remained blank. I was starting to wonder why I'd even brought it up. I should have just told Reagan that I had forgotten to ask Allie.

"No . . . I mean, yes, of course it's okay. We *are* just friends," Allie said, her face breaking into a smile. She sounded rattled, though. "Maybe it's just that now that I've moved and made new friends at a new school, and you guys are still at MLK, if feels a little weird when worlds collide. But that's okay! I just need to get used to it."

At that moment two customers walked in through the door, and I think all three of us felt relieved.

"Customers!" Allie said. "We can gossip more about the party later." She turned to help the man and woman, even though it was usually Tamiko's job to take the orders. "Welcome to Molly's!" Allie said cheerfully. "How can we help you today?"

Tamiko and I exchanged a look.

"To be continued, "Tamiko whispered to me.

I agreed. This wasn't the end of the Allie and Colin conversation.

CHAPTER NINE
A SWIRL OF CONFUSION

The rest of our shift was pretty uneventful. Tamiko came up with a great new special that she called the I Want S'more, which was graham cracker crumbles and melted marshmallow over triple fudge ice cream, and we ended up serving a bunch of them.

As Tamiko and I were getting ready to clock out and head home, we counted our tips from the tip jar and split them three ways with Allie. She was planning to stay on for a while and help her mom, since one of the college employees couldn't make it for another hour.

I thought about offering to stay and help too, but I really needed to get home and start my homework for the week. I'd been trying to get ahead on homework on Sunday nights so that I would have less on the days when I had both a sports practice and a Wildflowers rehearsal after school, and that had been helping a lot.

"I guess I'll see you next weekend," I said to Allie.

She was about to reply, when her mom came out from backstage with an envelope in her hand.

"Hi, girls! It sounded busy out here this afternoon. Was it a good day?" Her eyes scanned the tubs of ice cream and seemed pleased to see that a few were running low, particularly the triple fudge, which hadn't been selling very well before.

"I have exciting news," Mrs. Shear said. "Remember when I said I was going to start the Employee of the Month initiative? Well, it's officially begun!"

The three of us smiled at one another, waiting to hear who had earned it.

"This employee has truly been exceptional this month," Mrs. Shear went on. "She's been consistently on time, despite a truly busy schedule. Not only that, but she came up with a terrific new ice cream flavor—Coffee and Doughnuts! In a very short time it's become one of our most popular flavors, and I can hardly make the coffee ice cream fast enough."

I smiled at Tamiko, excited that she would be winning the award. She deserved it. She was always coming up with great new flavors. Mrs. Shear didn't even know yet about today's I Want S'more.

But then something happened that made no sense. Mrs. Shear extended the envelope to *me*. Me! The late one.

I froze. With everything going on, I had forgotten how Tamiko had covered for me that day when I'd been really late, how she'd said that the new flavor combo was my idea.

"Congratulations, Sierra," Mrs. Shear said. "It isn't a whole lot, but it's a thank-you for being such an excellent employee this month. Keep up the good work!"

I remained utterly frozen. I didn't even reach out for the envelope. I couldn't.

Mrs. Shear laughed. "What's the matter, Sierra? Go on. Take it!" she said, pressing the envelope into my hand. Then she turned to the other two girls. "Allie and Tamiko, I'm sure it'll be your turns soon." Then she looked at them expectantly, waiting from them to congratulate me.

"Oh yeah. Congratulations, Sierra," said Allie flatly.

Still Tamiko said nothing and just stared at me. I knew she was waiting for me to say something. I was waiting for me to say something too. I didn't know why my mouth wasn't opening.

"Tamiko?" Mrs. Shear said. "I understand that you might be a little disappointed, but please don't be. This is just the first of hopefully many Employee of the Month bonuses. It doesn't mean you aren't a stellar employee, just that Sierra did that little bit extra this month."

"I understand, Mrs. S.," Tamiko said evenly. "I can see how you'd think that. Congratulations, Sierra."

There was no mistaking the bitterness in her voice.

I didn't know what to do. I knew I had to speak up. I had to tell the truth! But I was afraid that if I did, and I admitted that Tamiko had covered for me that day and made up the Coffee and Doughnuts flavor herself, *and* that I'd been late a few of the other days as well, I'd lose my job.

And I couldn't lose my job! Lately it felt like it was the only thing holding my best friends and me together.

So I chickened out. Burning with shame, I ducked

my head and said, "Thank you, Mrs. Shear." Without looking at Tamiko or Allie, I fled outside with the envelope—and ran straight into Isa.

"Isa!" I exclaimed. "What are you doing here?"

Isa looked at me like I'd asked why the sky was blue, or why rain felt wet. "Uh, because *you're* here and I told Mom and Dad I'd come get you to meet them for dinner. Why? Am I not *allowed* to show up here when you're with your friends?"

"Of course you are," I said quickly. Poor Isa. She still looked miserable, and now I'd made her defensive. Whatever was bothering her, it was *really* bothering her. Molly's was a twenty-five-minute walk from our house.

Tamiko came out just then, and either didn't notice that Isa was there or didn't care, because she ripped into me. "Sierra! I can't *believe* you just did that! What is going on with you?"

I was about to reply and try to figure out a way to explain why I'd been such a coward and a bad friend, when Isa leapt to my defense.

"Don't you dare yell at her, Tamiko," Isa snapped. "She's been busting her butt to get here every week and make you guys happy."

Tamiko looked perplexed. Clearly she had not been expecting Isa to intervene. Neither had I.

I said, "It's not about being—"

"What do you care, Isa?" Tamiko cut in. "You don't even know what she did."

"I know you're not her *boss*," Isa replied.

What was going on here? Why were my sister and one of my best friends fighting? And in front of the store! I looked through the windows anxiously, hoping Allie and her mother wouldn't see this.

"Stop it, you guys," I begged. "Please. I don't want to get in trouble."

"Yeah—I kept you *out* of trouble," Tamiko said. She gestured at the envelope in my hands. "And there's the thanks I get."

"I had *no idea*, Tamiko," I replied meekly. "I—"

"C'mon, Sierra. Let's go," Isa snapped. "We're meeting Mom and Dad at Pino's Pizza for dinner. We're going to be late if we don't leave now."

"Just go," said Tamiko. "There's nothing for us to talk about anyway, Sierra. I can't believe you. We've been friends forever! You and Allie are the two people I trust the most in the whole world. You've really let me down."

I was so tired from my weeks of cramming in activities and trying to make everyone happy, and racing from here to there, that I just let myself be led down the sidewalk by Isa.

Could it have just been a coincidence that Isa had showed up exactly when I'd needed her? Or had it been our old twin-tuition?

I didn't know what was going on with Isa and me. But somehow, in the midst of whatever she was going through, and my crazy, hectic schedule, we were finding a way to lean on each other again. Before Isa and I arrived at Pino's to meet our parents, I tucked my Employee of the Month envelope into my pocket and vowed not to mention it. I knew I had to fix that situation, with both Mrs. Shear and Tamiko, and I wasn't sure yet what would be the best way to do it. I knew that if I told my parents about it, they'd use it as an opportunity to have yet another conversation with me about my schedule and commitments, and that most likely they'd make me quit the band. And I didn't want to quit anything! I wanted to continue to do all the things I loved, even if it meant that some nights I was staying up pretty late to get my homework done.

Isa was unusually chatty during dinner, particularly since she'd been so moody earlier in the day, so I let her carry the conversation. She seemed to like being the focus of Mom and Dad's attention, which made me wonder if maybe we spent too much time as a family talking about me and my activities. Isa wasn't involved in many things—she focused on soccer and spending time with her friends after school. And as long as her grades were good, our parents didn't interfere.

"Sierra, are you feeling okay?" Mom asked me as we were paying the check and getting ready to leave.

"Yes, I'm fine, Mami," I said. "Why?" I had been so careful all through dinner to smile and nod at the right times, to laugh when someone made a joke. Could she see what was going on in my mind?

My mother gestured at my plate, which had a single slice of pizza on it, and only a bite or two taken out of it. My salad was untouched. "You hardly ate! It's not like you not to eat Pino's Pizza."

She tilted her head to study me and quickly put a hand on my forehead. I brushed her hand off gently, saying, "No, Mami, I'm not sick. Just tired. And I had some ice cream earlier at work. That's all."

Isa raised her eyebrows knowingly, since she'd

witnessed some of the tension with Tamiko. But I was pretty sure she wouldn't mention that to our parents. She wasn't a snitch.

"Okay, if you're sure," Mom said. Then, "Is it your schedule that's worrying you?"

I couldn't help releasing a huge sigh. I was so tired of talking about this. "No, Mami, everything is fine. I just need to get home soon and start my homework."

I glanced at Isa, and she rolled her eyes theatrically at me. I wasn't sure if she was rolling them at our mother for worrying about me, or at me for not quite telling the truth.

Our parents paid the check, and the four of us left. The few bites of pizza I'd had sat in my stomach, heavy and greasy. The envelope in my pocket felt like it weighed ten pounds. I checked my phone constantly, hoping for a text from Allie or Tamiko, but nothing appeared.

I was miserable.

Immediately after we got home, I started my homework. I put the envelope on my dresser and sat on my bed and got to work. I started with English, trying to read some more *My Ántonia*, but the words kept going blurry, and then I would look over at my dresser and see the envelope sitting there. Why hadn't I just handed it over to Tamiko right then and there, when Mrs. Shear gave it to me? What must Allie and Tamiko think of me? Were they texting each other about me right now?

One thing was for sure—they weren't texting *me*. And that was very unusual for a Sunday night, when everyone was doing homework and getting ready for school the next day. Tamiko would often send us pictures of outfits she was thinking of wearing, and Allie would show us drafts of her upcoming Get the Scoop column for her school newspaper, where she reviewed books and recommended ice cream flavors to go with them.

I checked my phone for the ten thousandth time, but there was nothing.

Then, just as I was putting the phone down, it dinged that I'd gotten a new message. Breathless, I checked and saw that it was from Tessa.

Wildflowers—we need to have rehearsal at least one day this week! Our big performance is coming up! Can we all please find time for it?

She'd included lots of cute music emojis, but I

knew that the text was directed at me, because I was the one who had sports practices all week. Everyone was counting on me, so I would have to find a way. I'd have to skip something, or miss half of it, or I didn't know what. Because Tessa was right—we could not have our first gig and show up unprepared.

I texted back: No worries, Wildflowers! I'll find a time and get back to you ASAP!

Then I picked up my schedule and started looking. There was no space, really. No time available. Not with all of my school projects and softball and soccer and student council. I supposed I could miss the second half of soccer practice on Monday and go then. Maybe my coach would understand, since we didn't have a game this week.

I tossed my planner back onto my bed. I couldn't focus on that—not yet. First I needed some advice.

I went straight to Isa's door. I had my hand up to knock, but before my knuckles even touched the wood, Isa said, "Come in."

I opened the door, my mouth agape. "How did you know I was standing there? I tiptoed and hadn't even *touched* the door."

Isa was lying on her bed, exactly as I had been,

hunched over her math book. She shrugged mysteriously, keeping her face blank.

"Did you sense my presence?" I asked her, awed. "Was it our twin-tuition?"

"Must have been," she said. Then her face broke into a grin. "You should see yourself right now, Sierra! You look like you've seen a ghost." Then she cracked up, as if at some secret joke.

"What is it? Tell me!" I insisted.

Isa nodded her head toward Cinnamon, who was curled around one of Isa's feet. "You know how cats have better senses than we do? As soon as you were outside my door, Cinnamon turned to look at it and let me know someone was there."

She cackled again, and I had to laugh too. I was prepared to think Isa's and my brains were merging, and instead it was just her smart cat.

"So?" Isa said. "Are you going to tell me what's wrong?"

"You wouldn't tell *me* what was wrong with you earlier," I said.

Isa scowled. The dark, moody look that had been gone all through dinner came back. "That's because it's none of your business. But *you* came almost knocking on my door. So spill it, or let me get back to my homework."

"Okay," I said. "I did something really awful today."

"Oh?" she said, closing the textbook in front of her. "Well, now this is interesting. Go on. What'd you do? Lie? Cheat? Steal?"

I shook my head. "No, nothing like *that*," I replied. "Although, actually, *yes*, I did participate in a lie, and then I didn't speak up to correct it, so I guess I did lie twice. And maybe I did steal and cheat a little, because I got money for something I didn't do. Oh no! This is worse than I thought!"

I plopped down onto her desk chair and buried my face in my hands.

"Oh, relax, Sisi. Whatever you did, I'm sure it can be fixed. Everything can't always be happy and sunny in your world, you know. Occasionally you'll have to deal with some unpleasantness."

"This is more than unpleasant."

Isa waited, drumming her fingers on the hard cover of her math book. "I'm waiting. I can't help unless you're more specific. Come on, talk."

So I spilled the beans. I told Isa the whole story, from me being late several times, to the Coffee and

Doughnuts lie, to receiving the bonus today. And how Allie and Tamiko had been so stunned that I hadn't spoken up.

Isa looked at me thoughtfully. "I know how much you hate to get in trouble," she said. "So I can understand why you clammed up with Allie's mom. And you didn't know you were going to get the bonus. It's not like you planned to get it or anything."

"Yeah, but it's still wrong. And Tamiko is so angry!"

"Well, that's the easy part," Isa said. "You guys have been friends for years and years. You have nothing to worry about there. No matter what you did to Allie or Tamiko, you know that eventually they'll forgive you. You *might*, however, lose your job if you tell Mrs. Shear. Because she'll know you really don't have time to be there, and you lied to her, and she's the boss. So that's the real problem."

"They're both problems," I said.

"Yeah, but when you see Tamiko at school tomorrow, just explain that you were caught by surprise, and that you appreciate her covering for you, but you don't want to lose your job by telling Mrs. Shear. And then try to make sure she wins the award next month. I'm sure Tamiko doesn't want you to lose your job either. She'll understand. Friends cover for friends."

Isa sounded entirely confident in her plan, but for some reason it didn't sound 100 percent right to me. Tamiko had been really mad.

"So you're saying I just need to ride this out a bit, and it'll be okay?"

"Yes, although it's harder than it sounds," Isa said. "You're going to feel really uncomfortable for a few days. Tamiko might be snippy. But soon she'll see that correcting the mistake would make things worse for *both* of you, because she lied to cover for you, right? So really you're in this together. Allie, too, because she let you *both* lie to her mother. If you confess, you get all three of you in trouble."

Hmm. I hadn't thought of it like that.

"Knowing you, this whole thing will stress you out, because you like it when everyone loves you," Isa went on. "You probably won't sleep, or eat, or concentrate. . . . You'll fail a quiz—"

"Good grief, Isa! Stop!" I said, laughing. "I've been stressed out before. That's all I've been the past few weeks! I can handle a little more, I guess."

"Or you can just decide to not care what everyone else thinks, which is a lot easier," she said. "That's what I do."

I paused, thinking of her face earlier today. Whatever had happened, something or someone had hurt her. "Do you really not care what everyone thinks, Isa?" I asked her.

She drew her mouth into a tight line and frowned at me. "I really don't. I'm just me. Like it or not. Now, if we're done fixing *your* messy life, can you get out so I can do my math?"

CHAPTER TEN
WORST DAY EVER

Neither Allie nor Tamiko texted me Monday morning, either. So I repeated to myself over and over what Isa had said: *This will blow over. They'll get in trouble too if you tell Mrs. Shear. They're just upset now, but they'll get over it.*

I focused on my schedule for the week and on making sure I could fit in a band rehearsal. I found my soccer coach before first period and got her permission to leave practice a little early after school, then texted the Wildflowers that I'd be able to meet them at Reagan's around five. They all sent me happy faces and clapping hands. At least *they* still liked me.

Although, what if I hadn't been able to work it out and rehearse? Then would they have been mad?

Was there anyone who could deal with my crazy schedule other than me?

Later, as I was heading to my locker to grab my lunch, my phone dinged. I saw the name "Tamiko," and my heart leapt to my throat. She'd texted both me and Allie in our Sprinkle Sundays sisters group chat.

Don't sit with me and MacKenzie at lunch today, Miss Employee of the Month.

It took my breath away just to read it. I was used to Tamiko's bluntness, and in fact it was one of my favorite things about her, because whenever there was an issue among the three of us, Tamiko would bring it out into the open so that we could all resolve it quickly. But it really hurt to have it directed at me, and in front of Allie too. I wondered why she'd included Allie, since she wasn't at our school anymore and wouldn't be at lunch anyway.

I didn't know if I should text back. I started typing a few responses, but they were all pathetic, so I ended up not texting anything. Instead I had a brainstorm as I passed Claire Bright, the student council president, in the hallway.

"Hey, Claire," I said. "I know you wanted to have a

follow-up meeting about the spring fair. Any chance we can all meet at lunch today?"

Claire studied me for a second, hesitating about giving up her lunch period, I guess, but then she agreed. "Sure, Sierra. Great idea. I was hoping we wouldn't have to wait until next month's meeting to discuss it, because you know how long it takes to get volunteers signed up. . . ."

I let Claire keep talking and walked with her as we rounded up Vikram and Lee. Lee, predictably, was annoyed at us for taking up his lunchtime. But for me it was *way* better to be sitting with them having a meeting than to be sitting alone. If I had to do a little extra volunteering or student council work to make it up to Lee, I would. We found a table and got to work, me with a notepad taking the minutes since I was the secretary.

I glanced over at Tamiko and MacKenzie a couple of times. They had smooshed into the end of our usual table with some other girls. They were all laughing and joking.

At one point I got up to throw my trash out and turned around to see MacKenzie beside me, holding her trash as well.

"What's going on?" she asked. "Why aren't you sitting with us?"

I wasn't sure if Tamiko had said anything, and I was much too embarrassed to tell her the truth. So I said, "Nothing's going on. I just had a student council meeting." And I smiled brightly as if everything were perfectly normal.

MacKenzie looked doubtful. "Tamiko said you weren't sitting with us today. And she said it in a really weird way. Are you sure nothing's going on? Maybe I can help?"

I wanted to hug MacKenzie right there for being so nice and kind. But I knew Tamiko was watching, so I just said, "It'll all work out. I'll see you in science, okay?"

"Okay," MacKenzie said, walking away. She gave me one last look over her shoulder that let me know she still wasn't convinced.

I returned to my council meeting just as Lee was saying, "We need to meet about the fair again so we can make some final decisions about the theme. Can everybody do Friday after school?"

"I can't," I said. "I have softball." Lee looked annoyed, Claire sighed, and Vikram stabbed at his pasta angrily. For the first time, I couldn't help feeling like even *I* was getting a little tired of my busy schedule.

The day got worse from there. During my last-period study hall, I decided I couldn't stand the silence from my friends anymore. And I couldn't create impromptu student council meetings every lunch period either. I needed to stop waiting to be forgiven and use a different tactic. I would change the subject and try to get everyone to move on, just like Isa had said.

I texted both Allie and Tamiko and wrote: Hey, girls! Don't forget the bday party this Saturday night. The address is 97 Oak Ridge Drive. My dad can drive us there!

I knew there was a chance it wouldn't work, but I crossed my fingers and hoped for the best.

Allie wrote back a few minutes later with a thumbs-up, but then Tamiko immediately texted back: Seriously? You don't think I'm still going with you, do you?

I wasn't sure if she meant she wasn't going at *all*, or just not going to the party *with* me. Maybe she'd go with Allie. I knew Allie wanted to go because a bunch of Vista Green kids would be there, as well as kids from MLK. So she'd get to see some old and new friends. Plus, Colin would probably be there.

My band is playing, Tamiko. I'd really like you to come, I wrote back.

She replied: And I'd like my honest, trustworthy friend Sierra back. If you find her, tell her to call me.

Allie stayed out of it. I didn't blame her. I wanted out of it myself.

After school I went to soccer practice and played terribly. I completely missed the ball a bunch of times, and when I did connect with it, my aim was off. My teammates looked at me like I had five heads. And then when I had to leave early, I got more than a few dirty looks.

Apparently today was Everybody Hates Sierra Day.

It was a relief to get to Reagan's house and start rehearsing. At least none of the girls in the band were mad at me. Yet.

Then I started flubbing all of our songs. I knew the words—I'd memorized them—but I was so upset about Tamiko that I just couldn't remember anything.

I would start to sing, and I'd get the first verse out, and then my mind would go blank.

After the fourth or fifth time it happened, Reagan put her drumsticks down. She exchanged a look with Tessa and Kasey and said, "Girls, let's take five. Everyone, sit on the couch. Get some drinks, and we'll chill."

"But we need to rehearse," Tessa said worriedly. "We're going to be *in front of people* in just a few days."

"I know," said Reagan, "but right now we need to take five."

Gratefully I sank into the sofa and took a soda from the little fridge Reagan kept in the corner.

"So what's up with you?" Kasey asked, perched on the edge of the couch. Her bluntness reminded me of Tamiko. "You're a total mess today."

I hung my head. "I know—I'm so sorry. I'm just . . ." I couldn't bring myself to tell them how I'd treated one of my oldest friends, all because I hadn't bothered to prioritize my schedule properly. Because I was starting to realize that that was really what had happened. I'd been too busy being busy, and I hadn't put my job and my friends first, and the consequences were that I'd been late, my friend had covered for me, and I'd taken the credit for *her* smart idea.

I wasn't Sunshiny Sierra; I was Scummy Sierra.

"Well, whatever is going on with you, can you please work it out before Saturday?" Tessa said. "I *have* to make a good impression on Colin or else."

"Yes," I promised. "I will figure it out."

"Cooooolllllllllinnnnn," Kasey sang, with a laugh. "Tell us more about him, Tessa. What's he like? How'd you meet him?"

Tessa sighed audibly, a delicious contented sigh, like my cat Marshmallow made when I scratched her ears.

"I met him over the summer at the pool. He was with some friends, and I was with some friends. But then for some reason we kept bumping into each other. Like we'd both go to get Popsicles at the same time, or go to the diving well at the same time. And he said my pencil dive was really good—"

"You are a great diver," Reagan chimed in.

"Thanks!" Tessa beamed. "And I didn't feel that shy around him, the way I do around most people. Maybe because he wasn't loud and obnoxious like some boys. He was quieter, more serious. He has these really nice brown eyes and dark lashes. . . ."

I was starting to get yet another bad feeling in my stomach. Tessa *seriously* liked this boy. But what if Allie did too? What would happen at this party if Tessa and Allie were both there and Colin spent more time talking to Allie, his good friend from school? Would Tessa blame *me* for bringing Allie? Would it start even more friend trouble for me by making my band angry?

Maybe I shouldn't go to the birthday party at all. Maybe it would just make everything *worse*.

"Sierra, you look absolutely terrified right now," Kasey said. "Don't worry so much! You're just having an off day. When the party comes, you'll be ready. Just practice a lot at home this week. Sing everywhere, all day. I play on my desk at school like it's a keyboard and practice all my chords."

The others chimed in with their advice. I appreciated the sympathy, but the truth was, nothing was going to make me sing better at that birthday party except for one thing—being forgiven by my friend.

I'd tried it Isa's way for one very long and miserable day, and it had been too much for me. I couldn't "ride this out" and see if my friend forgave me. I'd done something wrong, and I knew it. And there was only one way out of it, even if it meant getting us all in trouble.

It was so simple. All I had to do was tell the truth.

As soon as I got home from band practice, I texted Allie and Tamiko. Will you both meet me at Molly's after school tomorrow? I made a mistake, and I want to make it right.

To my relief, Tamiko texted back almost immediately: K.

It was just one letter, but it meant everything.

A little while later Allie texted me privately: Tamiko says she's still not eating lunch w/u tomorrow. But you're both coming to Molly's after school?

I texted back: Yes. And I'll be there on time! I was going to have to skip softball to do it, but I knew that was the right thing. Especially when Allie texted me back with a smiley face and a heart.

111

CHAPTER ELEVEN

TRUE CONFESSIONS

I walked to Molly's after school the next day, rehearsing in my head what I would say. I was in trouble with my softball team for skipping practice, but I knew without a doubt that this was my top priority right now. When I'd gotten everything back on track with my best friends, then I could do damage control on the other areas of my life. But first things first.

When I arrived, Allie and her mom were behind the counter. Allie had obviously told her mom that I would be coming by, because instead of being surprised to see me, Mrs. Shear just said, "Well, hello, Sierra. Do you want anything while we wait for Tamiko? I made a new flavor last night—Lemon Licorice."

"No, thank you," I said. I had never in my life felt

less like eating ice cream. "I'm not hungry."

Tamiko walked in the door a minute later, but she and I didn't greet each other. She just stood, her arms crossed, staring at me. The tension was so thick that you could have cut it with a knife, and Mrs. Shear noticed.

"Girls, just *what* is going on here? Are you all about to quit?"

"No, no, Mom," Allie said anxiously. "Nothing like that." Then she looked at me, clearly wanting me to take charge and get this going. There were no customers in the shop at the moment, but it was still unseasonably warm out, so there were a few people eating cones at the tables out on the sidewalk, and they could come in at any time for a napkin or to use the bathroom or whatever.

It was now or never. I opened my mouth, and everything came out in a big, noisy rush. "Mrs. Shear, I'm very sorry to tell you this, but I haven't been honest with you. I was late several times, and then two weeks ago when I was *really* late, I brought the doughnuts as an 'I'm sorry' for Allie and Tamiko. And then Tamiko, who was being a very good and loyal friend, came up with the Coffee and Doughnuts flavor on the spot and said that *that* was why I'd bought them, just so I wouldn't get in trouble. And she let me have all the credit!"

Tamiko's face started to relax some, but her arms were still crossed. I knew I wasn't done.

"Anyway, she covered for my lateness, which I am *very sorry* about, and then *I* ended up being named employee of the month, when really I'm often late and she's the one with all the great ice cream flavor ideas. Tamiko should really be your employee of the month."

I fished into my pocket for the envelope I'd brought. I'd never even opened it, so I still had no idea how much money was inside.

"Please take this bonus back and give it to the right person," I said, holding it out to Mrs. Shear. Then I gulped in a big breath of air and said the last part, the hardest part, the part that I'd been rehearsing all the way to the shop. A few tears welled up in my eyes, and I worked hard to keep them from falling. "If you don't think I should work here anymore, I'll understand."

Mrs. Shear stared at me, and then at Tamiko, and then at Allie. "Well, girls," she said, accepting the envelope. "You could knock me over with a feather. Although, I suppose it does explain how weird you all acted when I gave this to you on Sunday, Sierra."

She paused. "Why didn't you tell me this then?"

Embarrassed, I looked at the floor. "I panicked. I was afraid you'd fire me, and then I wouldn't get to be here with Allie and Tamiko every week."

Mrs. Shear turned and handed the envelope to Tamiko. "I think this rightfully belongs to you, my flavor-idea genius. You're a loyal friend, Tamiko."

Tamiko accepted the envelope with a nod and a proud smile. "Thanks, Mrs. Shear. I love working here. And I love coming up with new flavors! I'd do it anyway, even without a bonus."

"I have to say one more thing," Mrs. Shear said. "This is a business, and you three are employees. You are friends as well, but when you're here, you're employees. And that means you follow a code of conduct. You arrive on time, you work hard, and you're honest. I know you three are more than capable of all of these things, which is why I expect to see you *all* here on Sunday on time. Okay?"

"Really, Mrs. Shear?" I asked. "Me too?"

Mrs. Shear grinned. "Oh, Sierra, you are a late cookie sometimes. I know that. But I also know that you stay to make up the time, and that when you're here, your cheerful personality, your lovely singing, and your impressive abilities on the cash register make you a real asset. The customers like you!"

Allie nodded. "They do, Mom! They're always complimenting her sunny smile and how quickly she makes change."

I shot Allie a grateful look.

"I have a feeling you'll be arriving on time from now on," Mrs. Shear said. "You learned a lesson the hard way, didn't you?"

"I definitely did," I said.

Mrs. Shear shooed us out from behind the counter. "Why don't you go outside and catch up for a bit, girls? I'll stay here and watch the counter. After all, none of you are working today."

"Thanks, Mom," said Allie, ushering us outside. I could tell she was relieved to have the conversation with her mom over with.

I was too, but there was still one more conversation to have. I hoped it would go as well as the first one.

The three of us plopped down at a table outside, and Tamiko ran her finger along the edge of the envelope. "You know I wasn't upset about the bonus money, right?" she said to me.

"Oh, I know that! I'm really sorry, Tamiko. What I did was wrong."

Finally Tamiko's face broke into its wide, familiar smile. "Why didn't you just say that right away? I would have forgiven you!"

I shook my head. "I don't know. I think . . . I think deep down I was a little mad at you and Allie maybe, for always making me feel bad about my other activities. Like I had to choose between them or you. When really, shouldn't I be able to do whatever I want? Don't you want me to be happy?"

Tamiko sighed. "Of course, Sierra! We do want that. I know how much you love softball, and soccer, and student council, and the play, and your band, and working here. Ugh! I'm tired just *listing* all the things you do. But I guess after you were late a few times, Allie and I were beginning to feel like we were your last-choice activity. And that hurt."

"Yeah," Allie chimed in. "Maybe we were a little jealous. You know everyone at school—and everyone knows you because you're so involved. Sometimes I worry you won't need us anymore. And I guess it felt to me like maybe you were taking our friendship for granted."

"I'm not! I would never do that!" I exclaimed.

"I'm so sorry I made you feel that way. Our friendship is my top priority—really."

Allie and Tamiko shared a look. "So you'd be willing to quit the Wildflowers for us?" Tamiko asked.

My jaw dropped slightly. Were they really asking me to give up my band?

"Um, well, I . . ." I didn't know how to respond. Was it fair of them to ask me to give up something I loved? Would I have asked them to do the same? Would I have asked Allie to give up reading, and writing her book review column in the paper, or asked Tamiko to quit cross-country or stop bedazzling everything in her bedroom?

No, I wouldn't have.

"Guys, I—" I started to say.

But Allie cut me off in a burst of laughter. "Sierra! Tamiko's *kidding*. We would never ask you to stop doing something you love. And we know you love the band. We'll just have to get used to sharing you, even if we'd prefer to keep you all to ourselves."

"Yeah," Tamiko agreed. "I don't like that you're so busy all the time, because I feel like you have less time for *me*. But I know it's what makes you happy. And that's what's important."

"Aw, guys!" I said, throwing my arms around them both. "Thank you! Thank you for understanding. I've got this scheduling thing down now. Really."

"Sure," said Tamiko, giggling. "And the sky is yellow. But listen. How about we stop talking and all go in and get some delicious Coffee and Doughnuts ice cream? I heard a real *flavor genius* came up with it. And I could use a little sprinkle of happy right now."

Allie squeezed my arm and said, "Personally, I'm in the mood for a forgiveness float."

"Me too," I said, feeling so relieved that I hadn't even realized I'd started humming.

"Hey, what's that song?" Tamiko asked me. "It's catchy."

I smiled proudly. "It happens to be a Wildflowers original by our guitar player, Tessa. We've been rehearsing it for Patrick's birthday party."

"Oh, I can't wait to hear you sing in front of people!" Allie said. "I'm going to be so, so, so proud."

"I guess I need to get back to work on my party outfit," Tamiko said. "Because I wouldn't miss your rock-star debut for anything!"

Sierra Perez, rock star. Rock star with two best friends, that is. I hummed a little more loudly.

CHAPTER TWELVE
BEST NIGHT EVER

A few nights later I hurried into my house, having just run home from soccer practice. It was already dinnertime, and I knew I'd be the last one to the table. I quickly washed my hands and then plopped down into my chair. Dad and Isa were already there, waiting for me.

"Sierra," Mom began warningly.

"Yes?" I asked.

I saw her hesitate, and I knew she was about to chide me for almost being late to dinner. But since no one had started eating yet, I technically wasn't late.

She exhaled and put her napkin into her lap. "Never mind," she said. "Glad you made it."

Since I'd started my rigorous scheduling system,

and was making it to *most* things on time, I'd noticed that I'd been getting a pass more from my family, and from my other activities. I'd apologized to my softball coach for missing practice the other day, and had offered to stay and help clean and organize the equipment after the next practice. And I'd just worked twice as hard in soccer as I normally did, to make up for having left early on Monday.

"I'm glad I made it too," I said honestly. "Dinner looks delicious, Papi!"

Dad had made his delicious chicken stew with pimientos, one of my favorites. Happy, I picked up my spoon and dug in. I was ravenous from soccer, and I'd never been a light eater. How could I be, growing up in a house with such yummy Cuban food?

"Your big band debut is this Saturday, right, Sierra?" Mom asked.

I nodded, swallowing what was in my mouth. "Yes—a boy from Vista Green is having a birthday party. Allie and Tamiko are coming too."

Isa raised her eyebrows. "So you guys made up? They forgave you?"

"What's this?" Dad asked. "Forgave you for what?"

I shot Isa a look. I didn't appreciate her mentioning

all that in front of our parents. I didn't tell them her private business (not that I knew any of it).

"It's nothing, Papi," I said. "We worked it out."

Isa snorted. "Yeah, but are they still trying to tell you what you can and can't do? Did you just spinelessly apologize and beg forgiveness, or let it blow over like I told you to?"

I took several deep breaths and reminded myself to remain calm. I had learned a thing or two these past few weeks about how to keep from feeling overwhelmed. "Isa," I said slowly, "I appreciate your advice from the other day. But in this case I was the one who was wrong, so yes, I did apologize. And I'm glad I did, because Allie and Tamiko and I had a really good talk, and we all understand one another better now."

Isa's face darkened, and she poked at her stew. "I just don't want them bossing you around, Sierra. Sometimes you're too nice."

"There's no such thing as too nice," I replied, and I meant it. I loved being a good friend. A good band member. A good employee! I never wanted to let anyone down.

"I think you need to fill us in," Mom said. "This

sounds serious, Sierra. Was the disagreement about working at Molly's?"

I shook my head. I really didn't want to get my parents involved, especially since I was proud of the way I'd handled it with my friends, and I didn't want more lectures on my activities. "Not exactly."

"Isa, I'm not sure what you and Sierra talked about," Mom said, "but let me be clear: in this house we ask forgiveness when we've done something wrong. Yes, you should expect that your friends and family will always love you, but you can't just let things blow over. Apologies help people forgive and forget."

"Why is everyone jumping all over me?" Isa complained. "I'm not the one involved in fifty different things and causing these situations in the first place."

Mom and Dad seemed to absorb that for a moment. Then Dad turned to me. "Maybe adding the band to your busy life isn't working," he said. "I know you always make homework your last priority, but in *this* house, academics need to be a top priority. Maybe you need to think about dropping something. Not necessarily the band, but something."

"Actually, Papi, my grades have been really good lately. I've started doing extra studying on Sunday nights, and making sure I write down all of my assignments in a chart." Then I put my spoon down and said the thing I'd been thinking ever since my conversation with Allie and Tamiko on Tuesday.

"I'd like to propose that as long as my grades are good, and I'm getting everywhere I need to be, that you let me do as many activities as I feel I can handle. After all, I'm the one who has to manage my time. And, well, my activities make me happy. I'm happy doing lots of different things. Even if that doesn't make sense to other people."

Everyone was silent for a moment. Then Mom put her hand on my shoulder and smiled proudly. "Well said, Sierra. And you know what? I think you're right. We shouldn't get to determine your schedule. You're in middle school. This is part of you learning to be independent."

Dad nodded. "I agree. How about you promise to come to us if you're in a bind and need help?"

"I will," I promised. "Now, can we talk about something else for a change?"

"Yes!" Mom agreed, and turned to Isa. "Are you

going to go to Sierra's musical debut Saturday? Papi and I will be there."

I froze. "Mom! No way," I said, hoping she was teasing.

"I'm kidding," Mom said, laughing. "I wouldn't do that to you. Maybe Isa can take a video for us."

Isa glared silently at her dinner, and I wondered why she wasn't responding. Then I realized something—I'd never invited her! I'd assumed she would never in a million years want to go to a birthday party that my friends and I were attending.

But maybe I'd assumed wrong.

"Do you want to come, Isa?" I asked.

She continued to stare at her food.

"I'd be happy if you were there. You could hang out with Allie and Tamiko."

Slowly Isa shook her head. "Thanks, Sisi. But I've got plans Saturday. Maybe another time."

I was disappointed, even though I hadn't allowed myself to get my hopes up that my twin would be there. There was something that kept Isa away from my group, and my friends, and I didn't know what it was. But if everyone was going to let me be me, then I knew I should let her be her.

"Okay, but if you change your mind, tell me. You can come with me and the band. You get special treatment because you're the sister of the lead singer!"

Isa cracked a smile, and we all went back to eating. I knew that Isa wouldn't make it to the party, but I had a feeling that she'd come to something in the future.

Saturday finally arrived. I'd let Tamiko pick out my outfit, which was what she called "rocker chic." I had on faded black jeans with some tears in the knees, black ankle boots, and a teal tank top of hers that she'd embellished with fringe and beads. I felt good in it, but it was a far cry from my usual long flowy shirts and cheery print patterns. My thick curly hair was loose and free, and Tamiko told me to shake my head around a lot. I had a feeling she thought the Wildflowers were a little more rock 'n' roll than we actually were.

I rode to the birthday party with the band, since Reagan's dad had a minivan and had offered to take us all. Earlier in the day we'd gone over and set up the drums and keyboard in Patrick's backyard.

Allie and Tamiko were already at the party when

the rest of the Wildflowers and I walked in. Tamiko was in the kitchen chatting with two girls that Allie had become friends with at Vista Green, while Allie was in the living room talking to a boy. As I moved closer, I could tell by his profile that it was Colin.

Uh-oh.

I glanced over at Tessa, who'd styled her dirty-blond hair in long loose curls down her back and was wearing jeans and a pink tee and pink lip gloss. She looked terrific. I found myself torn. I didn't know whether to hope Tessa would get the chance to talk with Colin, or to hope that Colin would spend the whole night talking to Allie.

Kasey hissed, "Is that him?" Tessa nodded silently. Even I could see the way Colin smiled at Allie as he talked to her, and she looked especially cute too, wearing another embellished tee by Tamiko.

Then Patrick yelled, "The band's here! Hey, guys, get ready! They're going to start playing soon!"

I glanced at my bandmates, and even Reagan looked slightly terrified. This had all sounded so fun when we'd been planning it in her garage. But now that we were here, in Patrick's house with all these kids staring at us, I felt the pressure.

I was the singer. What if I forgot all the words?

After years of best-friendship, Allie must have sensed how I was feeling, because she jumped up right away and came over to me. "Sierra! You're here! I'm so excited to hear you guys play. I'm Allie," she added as she turned to the other members of the band. Reagan and Kasey both said hi, but Tessa hung back, quiet.

I wondered if she'd realized that Allie was friends with Colin and was going to be rude and not say hello, but then I saw what it was that had made her so quiet.

Colin had gotten up with Allie and come over to say hi to us. I'd met him a few times at Molly's—he was a very loyal customer.

And right now his eyes were fixed on Tessa.

"Tessa!" he said. "Hi. I haven't seen you since—I don't know, a while. It's *your* band that's playing?"

Tessa nodded shyly, an unmistakable blush rising to her cheeks. "I play guitar," she said.

"I remember," replied Colin.

"She writes a lot of our songs too," Reagan chimed in. I hoped she wasn't going to say anything about "You're the One." I was pretty sure that Tessa would melt onto the floor or something.

Colin and Tessa chatted for a second, and Allie gave them an odd look, almost as if she couldn't understand what was going on. But when Tamiko came over to say hi, Allie's face was normal again, and she sounded like herself.

"Can we stand right up front while you play?" Allie asked.

"And scream?" Tamiko added. "I've got the flashlight on my phone all ready to go."

I laughed. "You can do ALL of those things. Just don't make me forget my words. . . . I'm so nervous!"

Tamiko hugged me. "You'll do great. You do everything great!"

I hugged her back. I hoped she knew how much those words meant to me. "Well, I'm not a flavor genius like some people, but thanks."

Kasey gestured at me wildly from the doorway. "Sierra, come on! We're going to go warm up."

Allie clutched my hands. "Good luck!" she said. "We'll cheer for you, no matter what."

"Um, thanks, I think."

I took a few deep breaths and followed my bandmates to the backyard. Patrick (or maybe his parents) had lit some Tiki torches around the yard, so it looked really pretty, and our instruments were set up on one side, so there was a lot of room on the stone patio for dancing. It was a really neat place to play, and I felt lucky to have this chance. So why was I so nervous?

We all took our places and began quietly warming up. Tessa strummed her guitar, I sang softly with no mic, Reagan played air drums, and Kasey turned the volume on her keyboard all the way down. After a few minutes of running through our first few songs, I felt more confident. We could do this.

Reagan looked at all of us. "Okay, Wildflowers. Are we ready?"

"YES!" Kasey shouted.

"Um, I think so?" said Tessa, and we all laughed.

Reagan gave the signal to her cousin, and Patrick ushered everyone outside. In seconds we had a backyard full of kids, all of them staring at us with anticipation.

Reagan banged her sticks together. "And a one, a two, a one, two, three, FOUR!"

And off we went. We started with an upbeat pop song to get everyone loosened up and relaxed. I kept my voice strong and confident, and stayed with the music. I saw Allie and Tamiko jumping around and dancing, and they both looked like they were having a great time.

A few seconds later, as we switched to another good dance song, I saw Colin appear to one side of Allie and begin dancing next to her.

Curious, I watched them, even as I was singing. When we'd first arrived, he had seemed really into Allie. Then he had looked really happy to see Tessa. But now here he was, dancing with Allie. Was he just the world's friendliest person? He was so hard to read!

I glanced over at Tessa and saw that she had noticed Allie and Colin dancing together. Her eyes looked big and sad, but she ducked her head and kept playing. When our song ended and we were supposed to move on to "You're the One," I turned around quickly to check in with everyone.

"Tessa, do you want us to play 'You're the One' now?" I whispered.

Reagan, who had also noticed Allie and Colin, said, "Yes, of course! He needs to hear it."

"No *way*," said Tessa.

"But it's on our song list!" said Kasey. "And we don't have many songs, especially slow ones. People are going to want to dance."

Tessa sighed. "Fine, but *don't* say I wrote it."

"Got it," I said, giving her a thumbs-up.

I whirled back around to the mic. I was starting to feel more comfortable in front of the crowd. In fact, I was having fun. This wasn't that different from performing in a soccer game or a play. But it was better, because I was singing.

"Next up we have an original song called 'You're the One.' And it's for all of you out there who have ever really liked someone. . . ."

Just as I said that, we started playing, and I saw Colin's eyes flash up toward Tessa. She immediately played a wrong chord.

I shook the thought away and focused on singing Tessa's beautiful lyrics. It really was a great song.

> *You're the one.*
> *I see you in my dreams.*
> *You're the one.*
> *But telling you is harder than it seems.*
> *You're the one.*
> *My love is deep and true!*
> *You're the one.*
> *But what if I'm not . . . not the one for you?*

The Wildflowers played, and everyone danced. When the song was over, everybody cheered. I saw Colin smile at Tessa and she smiled back. I relaxed a little bit because I realized that no matter who he ended up liking, Colin was a nice enough boy that he would make sure neither girl was hurt.

And I couldn't help thinking of how happy I was to be there, with my band and my best friends. Maybe I did do too many things, as everyone loved to tell me, but if I didn't, I wouldn't have moments like this. And I wouldn't have traded this for anything.

As we were finishing up the song, I saw my own face looking back at me from the far corner of the patio. It was Isa, and she was nodding her head to the beat.

At first I was surprised, but then I smiled and waved as I sang, and she waved back.

I had a feeling she'd disappear as soon as our set was over and not stick around to hang out with my friends. But it didn't matter. She had come to see me, because she was my sister and she knew how much I wanted her there.

How? Twin-tuition, of course.

When the song ended, all the kids burst into applause. "YOU'RE MY HERO, SIERRA!" Tamiko screamed over the noise. Allie jumped up and down, beaming. We sang a few more songs, and then it was over.

"All right, Wildflowers. We did it!" Reagan cried, and she pulled us all into a group hug.

I thought about how crazy the past month had been. Trying to arrange my crazy schedule, fighting with my BFF, becoming the lead singer in a band. It had been hectic and exhausting, but also a little bit exhilarating.

And I wouldn't have changed it for anything in the world.

DON'T MISS BOOK 7:

ROCKY ROAD AHEAD

It was the after-lunch rush on a beautiful Sunday afternoon—that's about as busy as Molly's Ice Cream shop ever gets, and I love it! I feel so good when we're busy—moving smoothly behind the counter with my friends Tamiko and Sierra like a well-oiled machine, the register ringing and ringing up sales, and inventory (as my mom calls our ice cream and toppings) moving out the door. Most of all, I love happy customers, and today we had plenty!

There was a group of Girl Scouts coming back from a campout. They were all hot and tired and wanted to be refreshed, so we sold them a lot of sorbet. There were grandparents babysitting grandchildren, and they always went big: unicorn sundaes, candy toppings, hot fudge—all the stuff parents usually forbade, the grandparents bought. Putting together the more complicated items on the menu satisfies our creativity as scoopers. After all, it's more fun to create a fancy mermaid sundae than it is to put a scoop of vanilla ice cream on a cone, even if it *is* rich, creamy, delicious Molly's Ice Cream vanilla!

My friends and I were in the middle of serving a car pool of Little Leaguers when I noticed my mom had come into the store from her office in the back. Her eyes were bright with excitement, and her cheeks were pink—she looked like she had news of some sort. I wanted to stop what I was doing and run over to talk to her, but we were too overwhelmed: the line was out the door. I was alternating between scooping and running the register, which meant I couldn't take a break for even one second.

I kept my eye on her as we worked through the rush. She went back to her office and returned with her laptop in hand, right as the line was drawing to an end. I caught her eye, and she grinned widely at me. Phew! That meant she definitely had good news. I was so eager to chat with her that I rushed as I packed a scoop onto a cone, and I cracked it and had to start over. Ice cream is the ultimate slow food—there's just no way to rush making it, serving it, or eating it!

Finally, finally, things died down, and I darted over to my mom.

"What's going on?" I asked breathlessly. "You look so excited!"

My mom smiled again and threw her arm around me in a sideways hug. "We're going to be famous!" she said with a laugh.

I laughed too, just because she was so happy. "How? Why?"

By now Tamiko and Sierra had wiped down the counters and joined us.

"Girls, I just got a wonderful e-mail from a reporter at *Yay Gourmet*, the online food magazine!"

"*Yay Gourmet*?!" Tamiko squealed. "I love them! Their site is supercool and amazing at predicting new food trends."

"And what did the e-mail say?" Sierra asked.

My mom beamed proudly. "They want to do a big article about Molly's!"

"Cool!" Sierra and I exclaimed together.

Tamiko clapped her hands. "What are they going to focus on in the article?"

My mom tipped her head to the side thoughtfully. "I think our flavors, most of all. Then our technique—the small batches, the high-quality ingredients, the test kitchen where I make everything. But there will certainly be a section on the wonderful concoctions you girls have created: the sundaes, shakes, and . . ."

"And the sprinkle of happy?" Sierra and I chimed in.

My mom laughed. "Of course! What would Molly's be without a sprinkle of happy?"

A sprinkle of happy is something we invented in the early days of the store last year, right when we all started working here together every Sunday. No matter how plain or complicated the ice cream order is, we put a pinch of rainbow sprinkles on top and say to the customer, "Here's a sprinkle of happy!" It started out as an accident, when Allie accidentally put sprinkles on a cone when the customer didn't ask for them. But it turned out to be a happy accident. People love it. It always, *always* makes them smile.

"When will the article run?" asked Tamiko. She's the person interested in details.

"I'm not sure the exact date," said my mom, "but I definitely think early summer. The reporter mentioned publishing it right in time for 'ice cream season.'"

Tamiko wrinkled her nose. "Don't they know it's *always* ice cream season at Molly's?"

Sierra and I laughed. Tamiko is a marketing whiz, and she loves trying to think of new ways to attract customers and attention: promotions, flyers, special events, social media, new menu items. She's a one-girl publicity machine, and Molly's has a lot to thank her for, especially building our fan base and attracting and keeping customers.

"We will make sure the reporter knows that before they leave the store," said my mom with a nod of agreement. "Ice cream's not just for summer anymore!"

My two friends and I went back to our spots behind the counter and began straightening up the chaos that our busy hour and a half had created. Sierra topped off the pots of sprinkles, toppings, and candies. Tamiko restocked cones, napkins, and cups. I refilled the crocks with marshmallow, hot fudge, and caramel (a sticky task!). As we worked, we discussed our summer plans.

"Are you going back to your sleepaway camp again?" Tamiko asked me.

I shrugged. "I'm not really sure. Things are different this summer, since . . ."

My friends knew what I meant: since my parents' divorce. At the end of last summer I had come back from my happy place (sleepaway camp) to discover that my parents were getting divorced and it was a done deal. They were both moving to new places, my brother and I were going to new schools, and my mom was switching to a new job, which was opening Molly's.

It had been a year of big changes and a lot more responsibility for me. But I also have much more independence now because of it. I get to work at Molly's, I sometimes take care of my brother, Tanner, I make us both dinner, and I get us off to bed, and my parents trust me to get around on my own more than they used to. Also, both of my parents now live in supercool, very different places that I love, and I got to start at an awesome new school. I still miss my old school—especially because Tamiko and Sierra are there without me—but I like a lot of things about my new school too, like the librarian, Mrs. K., and my English teacher, Ms. Healy, and being on the school paper staff, and my new friend Colin. Even the food is better at my new school.

Tamiko and Sierra and I have figured out how to

stay close even if we go to different schools, and that includes lots of video calls, working together every Sunday, rain or shine, and plenty of fun plans when we can fit them in.

But summer was still a big question mark. Would my mom need my help at home, watching Tanner, working at the store, or whatever? Would my dad want to spend more time together over the summer? Could we afford for me to go to that fancy camp up north for seven weeks again? We hadn't discussed it yet, but I wasn't even sure I *wanted* to go again. I almost hoped they'd make the decision for me. Or maybe that something better would come along.

"What about you, Sierra? Do you have summer plans?" I asked.

Sierra screwed the plastic lid back on the giant jar of rainbow sprinkles and stowed it in the cabinet. Straightening, she said, "Isa and I are going to work for our parents a bunch at their clinic. I'd love to work at Molly's, too. Maybe I could pick up some more shifts, what with summer being the busy season and me being free to help more."

I nodded. "That would be fun. The time will fly in here this summer because it'll be crowded all the time. What about you, Miko? Do you have a plan?"

"I have some DIY projects up my sleeve. I might get a table at the weekly flea market in the town square and sell some of my crafts and creations. Then my dad's talking about us all going to Japan in August to see my grandfather. I'd really be psyched to go," she said as she artfully created a pyramid display of cups of all sizes.

I clapped my hands. "Ooooh! That would be awesome! And maybe you could do some ice cream research there!"

"I know," said Tamiko, nodding. "Like the taiyaki!"

Taiyaki are little fish-shaped cakes that get filled with ice cream and dipped in fudge and sprinkles for decoration. Tamiko introduced them to Molly's, and now we run them as a special once a month.

"I'm sure you could learn new ice cream ideas without having to go all the way to Japan," offered Sierra as a new group of customers entered the store. "Welcome to Molly's!" she greeted them cheerfully, and we were off and running again.

After our shift was over, my mom told us each to help ourselves to a free treat since it had been such a busy day. I asked if we could borrow her laptop to look at the *Yay Gourmet* site while we relaxed, and she agreed, donning an apron and washing her hands to cover the pre-dinner lull before things heated up again later.

Sitting at a table in the far corner, we each indulged in our current favorite Molly's item. Tamiko was having a coconut cake sundae—coconut ice cream with yellow cake crumbles and real shredded coconut topping mixed in, all covered in a heavy pour of liquid marshmallow. Sierra had a simple dish of lemon sorbet in front of her. She felt tired and overheated and wanted to be refreshed, just like the Girl Scouts. I was hungry, so I went for something a little more satisfying: a Rocky Road cone that was crunchy, salty, and sweet.

Tamiko pulled up the *Yay Gourmet* site and began scrolling around. Sierra and I scooted our chairs closer to her so we could all look at the site together. It was such a pretty website, with a cool, puffy logo (it looked like it was made by a balloon artist) and brightly colored feature articles, with mouthwatering close-up photos and lots of handwritten notes and callouts with arrows. It made food look like the most fun thing on earth, which it kind of was!

"They have a cool take on food reporting," said Tamiko admiringly, scrolling through.

I nodded. "Yeah. It's like an annotated cookbook that a chef has had for years. Look at 'One Hundred Perfect Pasta Plates.'"

"And 'Crazy Potato Chip Flavors You Can Make at Home'!" said Sierra with a laugh, pointing at a sidebar.

"What will they say about Molly's, I wonder?" I said.

"'Artisanal Ice Cream Made by Geniuses'!" said Tamiko.

"'Made by *Beautiful* Geniuses'!" corrected Sierra.

We laughed.

"Or how about 'Beautiful, Well-Read Geniuses'?"

"'Beautiful, Stylish Geniuses'?"

"'Beautiful, Talented Geniuses'!"

As our laughter subsided, we took bites of our ice cream and ate thoughtfully while Tamiko clicked around the site. Suddenly, I felt a tiny bit of nervousness creep in.

"I hope they say nice things about Molly's," I said.

"Oh, please. How could they not?" said Tamiko with a shrug.

I raised my eyebrows. "Well, you never know. I mean, it's a free press. They could say anything about us. It's a little scary, actually."

"It's not really a *review* site, though," said Sierra. "It's not, like, the local paper, here to give us only one star or something."

"Hey! The local paper gave us five stars! The most we could get!" I pretended to look offended.

"Down, girl!" said Tamiko through a mouthful of coconut. "It's food news. And we've got plenty of *new* stuff going on here for them to write about. Get it? *NEWS*?"

"I guess," I said.

Sierra patted my back. "Don't worry. It's going to be great."

I smacked my forehead as I stood waiting for the school bus Monday morning. I'd forgotten to ask my mom if it would be okay for me to tell people about the *Yay Gourmet* article. I mean, I'd told my dad when he and Tanner came to pick me up for dinner after work at Molly's last night, but he was family.

The person I was most excited to tell was Colin, my school bus buddy and probably my closest friend at Vista Green, my new school (which wasn't that new to me anymore). He was the assistant editor of the school paper—actually, he was the person who'd encouraged me to join in the first place—and I knew he'd be interested in the *NEWS*, as Tamiko had called it.

The bus pulled up and I climbed aboard, scanning the crowd to find Colin sitting in one of our usual spots toward the back right. I passed the Mean Team—Blair, Palmer, and Maria—near the front and didn't even flick my eyes toward them. One-on-one, Maria could be okay, but Blair and Palmer were awful, and as a threesome they were intolerable. Colin had helped me deal with them right from the start.

Now Colin was smiling and waving me back. I smiled in return and beelined toward him, flopping into the seat and dropping my already-heavy backpack on the floor.

"Good weekend?" he asked, by way of greeting.

I tipped my head. "Weekends are always good. Better than weekdays, for sure."

He nodded, still smiling. "Totally. What did you do?"

I filled him in on my weekend, which didn't end up sounding that interesting because the one piece of information I was dying to share had to be carefully left out. Colin had had a decent weekend, but he'd had a lot to write and edit for the paper.

"You should consider writing more articles in the newspaper," Colin said. "My sister always says that you're the strongest writer on the staff."

I blushed. "Your older sister? The one who goes to high school?"

Colin laughed. "The one and only!"

"How does she know my writing?"

"I always bring home the school paper, and since she writes for the high school paper, she always checks it out. She loves your ice-cream-and-book pairings every week and says you're a really strong writer."

"Huh!" I sat back in my seat and looked away, pleased.

"She says most of my friends write well, but you stand out."

I turned to look back at him. "How does she know we're friends?" I blurted, and then regretted it as Colin blushed and looked out the window.

"Oh, I've just mentioned you at home. You know."

I knew. I'd mentioned Colin at home too. My family knew him first as "the boy who was nice on the bus my first day," and then "the boy who got me involved with the school paper," and finally "my friend Colin."

"My family knows you're my friend too," I offered.

"Thanks!" he said, turning to look at me. Then he squinted at my head. "New headband?"

I *was* wearing a new headband—brown with white polka dots—but I couldn't believe he'd noticed.

"Yes! What do you think?" I asked, jokingly making a fish face and turning my head at all angles like a model.

He laughed. "Headband-y," he said.

I punched him in the arm, not hard. "That's not even a word!"

"No, no, it's nice. You look good," he said, meeting my eyes.

I smiled and looked down as my cheeks grew pink. "Thanks."

When I went to the bathroom in between classes, I took an extralong look at myself in the new headband, turning my head back and forth and not caring who saw. Colin had liked the way it looked, and that gave me a new perspective. I'd never thought of him as someone who'd notice what I was wearing. Maybe being a newspaper editor made you more observant or something.

Later, walking down to the library after lunch, I spied myself in the reflection of one of the library's huge glass walls, and I caught myself smiling as I walked toward my own image. I had to laugh. I was acting like one of the Mean Team girls myself, smiling at my own reflection!

I had twelve minutes before my next class, and I wanted to say hi to Mrs. K., my favorite staff member at school, and also take a minute to look at some food magazines, if they had any.

"Hi, Mrs. K.!" I whispered as I entered the library.

"Oh, yes. Mm-hmm. Hello, dear. I know I have something here for you. Let's see." Mrs. K. rummaged through some small, neat piles on her full but tidy desk. She was always a fashion plate. Today she was wearing a navy-and-white-striped cotton boatneck sweater with long sleeves, navy capri pants, and black ballet flats, with her long dark hair in a ponytail.

"I like your outfit," I whispered.

"Thank you, dear. Feeling summery! Aha! Here we go. Yes." She handed me a stack of cookbooks. "Could you please shelve these for me? They're in one of your sections."

"Okay." I helped Mrs. K. maintain the bookshelves in our library. I was a volunteer, but it never felt like work for me. The library had been my haven when I first started here at Vista Green, and I'd do anything to give back. "Do you have any cooking magazines?" I added.

"Mm-hmm. Right over there at the far left of the periodical wall. Not a lot. Just some for the kitchen staff and our foodie teachers. Take a peek."

"Thanks." I crossed the plush rug that helped hush the room as I headed first to unload the cookbooks. There were only seven of them, and it was a small section, so it wouldn't take more than a minute. But midway through the stack, one of them caught my eye. It was called *Professional Food Photography*, and it had a photo of an ice cream sundae on the cover! I had to check this book out myself.

Quickly I shelved the last two books, and then I went to look at the periodical wall. Unfortunately, periodicals can't be checked out—they're too vulnerable to ripping and have a short shelf life—so I grabbed three magazines and sat in an armchair to flip through them for my remaining time.

The first one was for casual cooks looking for shortcuts: time-saving, money-saving, environment-saving recipes galore. It wasn't really what I was looking for. The next one was a majorly gourmet magazine featuring complicated multipart recipes that called for people to make their own sub-ingredients first (like homemade mayonnaise and chicken stock). Bor-ing! But the third magazine was a little edgier, closer to *Yay Gourmet*'s style and interesting, too.

Inside were articles like I'd seen on the website yesterday, many of them featuring gourmet shops and restaurants from around the country. They'd do a little profile of the chef or owner of a store, and then talk about the menu and the recipes. I kept flipping through the magazine and somehow ended up on the "Letters to the Editors" page. There, my eyes widened.

Three of the six letters were from people who wanted corrections to their articles. One mentioned a recipe that had been miswritten and resulted in a disgusting dish. Another said the magazine had misquoted her. And a third said the magazine had "willfully maligned" her business, which I took to mean criticized it too much. *Eek!*

For each letter, the magazine's editors apologized. I supposed it was good they admitted their mistakes and published them like this, but still—how many people had seen the original articles and been misled? How many of those would ever see the corrections?

I sat back in my chair and stared into space. My mom would have to be very careful about what she said in her *Yay Gourmet* interview. So would my friends and I. I wouldn't want Molly's to be a victim of these sorts of reporting errors. I was still super-excited for my mom, but now I felt a little nervous about releasing Molly's to the world on the internet and having no control over what was said about it. Maybe it was better to be small and *not* well known, if at least you could be sure you were in control of what was being said about you or your business.

The bell rang, and I quickly returned the magazines to their display area and presented the food photography book to Mrs. K. to check out. With a wave and a promise to return tomorrow, I dashed up the stairs to my math class on the first floor, the book clutched under my arm.

Math was fine, but I was distracted by the things I'd read in the library and eager to start flipping through the food photography book I now had. By the end of class, I was counting the hours until I could go home.

"Hey, Allie," said a voice.

I looked up from repacking my backpack. It was Patrick Ryan, a boy whose birthday party I'd attended recently. Sierra's new band had been playing at the party because the drummer, Reagan, was Patrick's cousin. She'd invited Tamiko and me and her twin, Isabel, so we could see her play, and there ended up being lots of kids there from Vista Green—including Colin! It was really fun.

"Hey, Patrick! I've been meaning to catch you to

say thanks for the party invite, but I keep missing you and I don't have any of your contact info."

"Thanks for coming! Small world, right?"

"Totally!" I agreed.

Patrick and I strolled out of math class and realized we were headed in the same direction, so we chatted as we walked.

"The Wildflowers are awesome, don't you think?" I asked. That was the name of Sierra's band.

"Yeah, I really couldn't believe it. I mean, Reagan's always been musical, but to see them come together so well—it was impressive." Then Patrick glanced at me. "Are you friends with Tessa, who writes the songs? The one who likes Colin?"

Wait, *what*? My heart skipped a beat. Tessa was the guitarist in the Wildflowers, and Sierra had told me that she had a crush on Colin. But how did Patrick know about it?

"Um . . . n-no?" I stuttered. Then I added awkwardly, "She seems nice?"

"Uh-huh. I only talked with her a little bit, but she seems supercool, don't you think?"

"Oh, yeah. I . . . barely met her."

"She and Colin would make a cute couple. I'll

have to dream up some other reason to have a party with a band so we can get those two together again." Patrick stopped outside the science lab. "Well, this is me! See you next time we have math!"

My head was spinning. I'd heard from Sierra that Tessa liked Colin, but I hadn't thought Patrick would know about it. Did Colin know about Tessa's feelings too? Did he like her back?

I sighed. Not that it mattered who Colin liked. Right?

But if so, then why did my conversation with Patrick leave such a bitter taste in my mouth?

Colin had chess after school today, so he wasn't on my bus home, thankfully. I was having trouble processing this new image of Colin and Tessa as a possible couple. It didn't match with the Colin who'd made me feel so good about my headband this morning. I was feeling . . . weird, I guess. I flipped through the food photography book on the bus a little bit, but I couldn't read it while we were in motion or I'd get carsick.

Once I was home, though, I curled up on the window seat in my room—a window seat never gets old—and I read through the photo book with my cat, Diana. But what I learned made me even more nervous about the *Yay Gourmet* feature than before!

It turns out that food photographers use lots of tricks of the trade to make food—or, I should say, "food"—look appealing. For example, droplets of milk are often actually Elmer's glue. Chicken breasts are often painted by hand to make grill marks. Stylists use red lipstick to brighten strawberries and use mashed potatoes to thicken milkshakes. Worst of all: vanilla ice cream is usually just white lard—animal fat—scooped from a bucket with an ice cream scooper.

The book said ice cream is the hardest thing of all to photograph because it melts under the lights. As soon as you get something that looks delicious and perfect, you have to light it with hot studio lights, and everything melts!

At that, I closed the book in disgust.

Scoops of lard at Molly's?

Never!